Hot Off The Red Carpet

By

Paige Tyler

Published by Blushing Books®,
a subsidiary of
ABCD Graphics and Design
977 Seminole Trail #233
Charlottesville, VA 22901

The trademark Blushing Books® is registered in the US Patent and Trademark Office.

Tyler, Paige
Hot Off The Red Carpet
eBook ISBN: 978-1-60968-893-6
Print Book ISBN: 978-1-60968-903-2

Cover Design: by ABCD Graphics

Korey Mae Johnson, Melinda Barron, Loki Renard ... they're all here, plus many more.

Embrace the spank!
See the stories first at The Woodshed!
http://www.herwoodshed.com

Paige Tyler

Visit her website here:
http://paigetylertheauthor.com/

Visit her blog here:
http://paigetylertheauthor.blogspot.com/

Books you might also enjoy by Paige Tyler are:
Nosy By Nature
The Cutler Brosthers Trilogy
Spanking Sydney.

Chapter One

Breathe, Addison Mattingly told herself. But the whole in-through-nose-out-through-mouth thing was a little hard to do when she was sitting in front of the palatial Beverly Hills home of the hottest actor in Hollywood, Trevor Braden.

She still couldn't believe the guards at the gate had let her in. She'd been sure the men would see right through her charade. In all honesty, she was still a little bit afraid the cops might show up and drag her off at any minute. Then again, the guards really didn't have any reason to suspect she wasn't who she said she was. Her name was listed on the access roster as Trevor Braden's new personal assistant, after all.

Okay, to be honest, her name wasn't on the access roster – her sister's was.

Her twin sister, Madison - the perfect one - had gotten the job as Trevor Braden's personal assistant. She always got everything she wanted, usually with little effort on her part. It had been like that from the time they were little. Everything just seemed to go the other girl's way. Of the two of them, Madison had always gotten the higher grades, the cuter boyfriends, the better job offers. She had "over-achiever" stamped all over her resume. When she had applied for the position as Trevor Braden's personal assistant, it had been on nothing more than a whim. But of course, she had gotten the job. She hadn't even had to go to LA for a face-to-face interview with the actor. Her resume was so impressive that his manager had hired her over the phone.

While Addison had stopped being jealous of her sister's accomplishments a long time ago, the fact that Madison had managed to land this job had really hurt. Addison idolized Trevor Braden. Well, maybe not idolized him. But she definitely had a huge crush on the man, and Madison knew it. To think that her sister would be spending practically every waking hour with the gorgeous movie star had almost been enough to make Addison scream.

But then, two days before she was supposed to move down to LA, Madison had decided she didn't want the job anymore.

"Sure, Trevor Braden is a hottie," she'd told Addison. "And while being his personal assistant would have its perks, I don't feel like spending my time babysitting some spoiled Hollywood actor. Where's the long-term potential in that?"

Then Madison had announced she'd taken a job as a personal assistant to some two-hundred-year-old Wall Street banker instead. Addison had just stared at her sister in disbelief, unable to believe that she would give up the chance to work for Trevor Braden. But apparently, Madison had visions of Manhattan penthouses, stock options, and a corner office at a prestigious big name firm. Who cared if the guy she was going to be working for was old enough to be her grandfather?

"If you think being Trevor Braden's personal assistant is so great, why don't you do it?" Madison had sneered. "Oh, I forgot. You couldn't get the job – not even in your dreams."

A few hours later, Madison had left for the East Coast, but not before she'd asked Addison to call Trevor Braden's manager and tell him that she had changed her mind about taking the job.

But Addison hadn't called. Deciding that she'd had enough of her sister's gloating, she had put on the only suit she owned, thrown the rest of her clothes in a couple of suitcases, and driven down the coast to Los Angeles.

Now, sitting in front of his house in her rather beat up Camry, she was too petrified to move. What the hell had she been thinking? She couldn't pull this off. She didn't know the first thing about being a personal assistant. Before she'd left San Francisco, she'd done some research on the Internet to get an idea of what the job entailed, and from everything she'd read, it sounded more than a little demanding. Madison might be a Grade-A bitch most of the time, but she had been right about one thing. Addison could have never gotten this job on her experience.

Though Addison had gone to a good college, it hadn't been the Ivy League school that her twin had gone to. And whereas her sister had known exactly what she'd wanted to do, Addison had taken a little of everything. While she had enjoyed it, she'd ended up graduating with what amounted to a four-year liberal arts degree. Though it was nothing to scoff at, it hadn't helped her figure out what she wanted to do with her life.

So, while her sister had gone on to get her Master's degree in business administration, which had led to a very prestigious intern position, Addison had moved from one job to another after college. Even now, at twenty-eight, she still wasn't sure exactly where she was headed. But she was damn sure she was going to like it when she got there.

Addison looked up at the huge, two-story house again and debated about what she should do. Common sense told her she should turn the car around and go back home to San Francisco. But how could she pass up an opportunity like this? If she left, she knew would end up regretting it for the rest of her life. On the other hand, if she stayed, she ran the risk of completely humiliating herself in front of Trevor Braden. She cringed at the thought.

Chiding herself for being such a coward, she started to turn the key in the ignition when a flash of movement in one of the upstairs windows caught her eye. She blinked. Oh God. It was him. Trevor Braden. Had he been pulling on his shirt? Was he just getting dressed? Or better yet, undressed? She blushed at the image that thought conjured up.

Before she even realized what she was doing, Addison was out of the car and hurrying up the front steps to ring the doorbell.

Unable to believe she was really doing this, she stood there holding her breath, her pulse racing. She should have run a brush through her hair before she got out of the car, she thought. And checked her make-up, too. God, she hoped she looked all right. But before she could think about it anymore, the door swung open.

Addison had expected a maid to open the door. Maybe a butler. Or even a bodyguard. Heck, even his manager. Anyone but Trevor Braden himself.

But there he stood. All mouth-watering, six-foot-four inches of him. And even more gorgeous in person.

She'd known he was tall, of course, but in real life, he seemed taller. His shoulders seemed broader, too. And his soulful dark eyes a more golden brown. His dark hair was slightly tousled as if he'd just run his fingers through it, and there was a slight scruff of beard outlining that amazingly chiseled jaw. He hadn't bothered to tuck in the button-up shirt he was wearing, and beneath his jeans, his feet were bare. She'd been right. He had been getting dressed.

"Hi," he said, giving her a smile. "Come on in."

Addison blinked. Trevor Braden, the most gorgeous, in-demand, sexiest hunk in Hollywood had just spoken to her. And she was just standing there staring at him like a dufus.

When she didn't reply, his brow furrowed. "You are Madison Mattingly, right? My new assistant."

"Addison," she automatically corrected. She was so used to people getting them mixed up that she'd done it without even thinking.

His frown deepened. "Oh. Sorry about that. I thought Murray said your name was Madison. I must have misheard him." He flashed her another grin. "And I'm usually pretty good at remembering names. Comes with the job."

Addison would have laughed at his joke, but she was too busy calling herself an idiot. How the heck could she expect to pull this off if she was already making mistakes like that? Crap! But she supposed it was too late to backtrack now. Even if she could, though, she wouldn't. For some ridiculous reason, she wanted Trevor Braden to call her by her own name instead of her sister's.

"It's Addison, actually," she explained, giving him a smile. "But it's easy to see how he could have mistaken it for Madison."

Trevor nodded. "Addison it is then." He took a step back. "Come on in."

Addison took a deep breath and stepped into the entryway. The inside of the house was as beautiful as the outside. Though obviously expensive, it wasn't ostentatious at all. Instead, it was decorated in sleek, modern lines. Designed with an open floor-plan, it had two sweeping staircases that met in the middle and underneath them, Addison could see a set of French doors. Beyond that, there was a huge patio with a beautiful swimming pool.

"So, how was the drive down?" Trevor asked as he shut the door.

She turned to look at him, her pulse skipping a little at his words. Good heavens, from the way her body was reacting, you'd think he'd just asked her go to the Oscars

10

with him or something. He was only making small talk, for heaven's sake.

Addison reached up to tuck her long, blond hair behind her ear. "Fine, thanks."

He nodded. "That's good. Well, if your car is unlocked, I'll go grab your bags and bring them up to your room."

She looked at him in surprise. Hollywood actors didn't offer to carry suitcases for the hired help. Or at least she'd never thought they did.

Abruptly realizing he was still waiting for an answer, she opened her mouth to tell him that she could bring in her bags herself when a man's voice interrupted her.

"Don't be silly. That's what Bob's here for, Trevor. He can go out and get them."

Addison saw Trevor's mouth tighten at the words and she turned to see two men walking into the entryway. One was tall with dark hair and built like a football player; the other was closer to her height, bespectacled, and didn't look athletic in the least.

The man with the glasses held out his hand. "You must be Madison. I'm Murray Siedle, Trevor's manager," he said. "We spoke on the phone."

She reached out to shake his hand. "It's Addison, actually," she said.

The small man looked at her in confusion for a moment, and Addison felt herself tense. But then he laughed, much to her relief. "I must have gotten your name wrong, I guess. Sorry about that." He glanced at Trevor. "I'm going to go get Addison up to speed. Let Bob get her bags and take them up to her bedroom, would you?"

Trevor looked like he wanted to say something in reply to his manager's words, but Murray didn't give him a chance. Instead, the man took Addison's arm and hurried her toward the back of the house. She barely had time to glance over her shoulder at Trevor before Murray hustled her into a room and shut the door.

Addison tottered a little on her four-inch heels as she came to a stop. She looked around the room and saw that it was an office, and a very well-equipped one at that. She wondered if it was Murray's or hers. Did a personal assistant even have an office?

Murray walked over to the desk. "Your resume is very impressive, Addison," he said as he picked up a thick leather-bound book. "Trevor's going to be in good hands with you, I know it."

She felt herself blush at the less-than-professional image the manager's words conjured up.

Murray didn't seem to notice her heightened color as he flipped through the day-planner in his hands. "Everything you need is in this book, so familiarize yourself with it. It has all the important contact numbers, as well as Trevor's schedule. He has two appointments this evening. One is a talk-show interview at a studio down in Burbank in a couple of hours, and the other is back here later tonight. He's meeting with a director about a new movie."

Trevor was making a new movie? She hoped it was one of those action/adventure flicks where he took his shirt off a lot. Those were her favorites. Before she could ask, though, Murray continued.

"For the interview in Burbank, you'll need to coordinate with his driver so make sure you do that right after we get done here. He's usually out back in the cottage. Or you can call him if that'd be easier. The number's in the book," he said. "I don't know if you did this kind of stuff at your previous position, but just give him the standard info. The pick-up and drop-off times on the sticky note there. Which studio you're going to. Things like that. Oh, and make sure to check that the limo is well stocked with Dasani Lemon. Trevor prefers it to the regular and I think that damn driver is sucking it down himself."

Dasani Lemon, huh? That was a new tidbit of information about Trevor that she didn't know. And she thought she knew everything about him!

"When you get to the studio, take Trevor to his dressing room, and then talk to the producer doing the show, make sure he knows which questions are out of bounds," Murray continued. "Get with stage manager, too. Trevor hates having studio lights pointing right in his eyes. Oh, and no autographs afterward. Trevor will want to sign them, but don't let him. He's on a tight schedule and I don't want him late for his meeting with the director. Speaking of which, tell the cook not to make any kind of hors d'oeuvres that have seafood in them. The director has some sort of thing against fish and won't touch the stuff. Piss off the director and Trevor can kiss the part goodbye."

* * *

Addison felt like her head was spinning. She was just thinking that maybe she should ask Murray to run through the list if instructions again so she could take notes when the manager announced that he needed to get with Trevor about a photo shoot he'd set up.

"Oh, by the way," Murray added as he left. "Your bedroom is just down the hall from Trevor's. Bob will show you where it is. If you need anything, my number is in the book."

Addison was so excited about her bedroom being down the hall from Trevor's that she barely heard the rest of what Murray said. Not only would she get to see the gorgeous Trevor Braden every day, but she'd get to sleep right down the hall from him. If she weren't so afraid someone might see, she'd do a little happy dance right there in the office!

Abruptly remembering the day-planner she was holding, Addison paged through it until she found the number for Trevor's driver. He answered right away and she gave him all the necessary information. She even remembered to mention the part about making sure the bar in the limo was stocked with Dasani Lemon.

Thinking that she should probably take Murray up on his suggestion to familiarize herself with Trevor's schedule, she took a few minutes to look through the day-planner. There were talk-show appearances and photo shoots mixed in with his regular filming schedule, plus some red-carpet events, including the premiere for his new movie. God, he was really busy.

A knock interrupted her and she looked up to see Bob standing in the open doorway. "Sorry to interrupt," he said. But Murray wanted me to show you to your room."

"Oh, okay." She closed the day-planner and slipped it into her shoulder bag.

"I'm Bob Davitt, by the way," the big man said as she stepped out of the room. "I'm Trevor's bodyguard."

From the way he was built, Addison should have guessed. "I'm Addison Mattingly," she said, and then realized he probably already knew that. She reached up to tuck her long, ash blonde hair behind her ear. "Thanks for bringing my bags up to my room."

"No problem," he said. "I'll give you a quick tour of the house on the way. That way you'll know where everything is."

The house was so big that Addison thought she might actually need a map to find her way around it. In addition to the spacious and very plush living room, there were three formal dining rooms, a huge gym, a media room that could have doubled for a movie theater, a recreation room with a pool table and video games, and another office like the one Murray had taken her to, not to mention more bedrooms than she could count.

When they stopped by the kitchen, Bob introduced her to the cook, Maribel. Or personal chef, as Bob called her. Plump with dark hair that had gone gray in places, the other woman gave her a warm smile and told her that if she needed anything, she should just ask. It wasn't until Bob was leading her upstairs a little while later that Addison remembered what Murray had said about the hors d'oeuvres. Rather than go back right then, Addison decided that she'd just stop by and talk to Maribel about them before she and Trevor left.

The bedroom Bob showed her to was huge, not to mention absolutely beautifully decorated, and Addison couldn't help but gasp. Her entire apartment would fit in here. Okay, maybe that was an exaggeration. But the room really was big.

"If you need anything, just yell," Bob said before heading back down the hall.

"I will," Addison said. She started to close the door, but then poked her head out. "Bob?"

He turned.

"Do you know where Trevor – Mr. Braden – is? We need to leave for the studio soon."

"He's probably in his bedroom getting ready," Bob supplied. "Two doors down that way," he added, gesturing with his finger.

She nodded. "Thanks."

Addison started to shut the door, but then hesitated. Maybe she should check in with Trevor. Just to see if he was actually getting ready. She didn't want them to be late, after all.

Smoothing her hands down the front of her skirt, she made her way down the hall to his room and knocked on the door. "Mr. Braden, it's Addison," she said.

"Come in," Trevor called.

Addison had to bite her lip to stifle a moan. God, he had a sexy voice! Taking a deep breath, she turned the knob and pushed open the door.

Trevor was standing in the middle of the room, dressed in a pair of jeans and nothing else. Whatever Addison had been going to say fled her mind at the sight of his bare chest. She'd seen him without a shirt in movies and magazines, of course, but they paled in comparison to the real thing. Damn, he was built!

"Which one do you think?" he said.

She was vaguely aware of him holding up a shirt in each hand, but she was too mesmerized by his chiseled chest and washboard stomach to even glance at them.

"Addison?"

She dragged her gaze away from his incredible body to find him regarding her curiously. "Wh-what was that?" she asked.

"Which shirt do you think I should wear for the talk show?" he asked.

Addison barely glanced at them. "Th-the dark blue," she stammered.

Trevor regarded it for a moment, and then shrugged. "I was kind of leaning toward the other one, but I think you're right." He flashed her a grin that made her pulse flutter. "I'm lousy at this type of thing."

Addison watched as he tossed the other shirt on the bed and shrugged into the one she'd picked out, wondering why he even bothered wearing one at all. Heck, with a body like his, he should just go shirtless all the time.

"So, what can I do for you?" he asked as he buttoned his shirt.

For starters, he could sweep her up in his arms, set her down on the bed, and make mad, passionate love to her. She imagined him ripping her clothes off like the guys always did in the romance books. The image brought a

16

rush of color to her cheeks, not to mention a delicious, little tingle to her pussy, and she almost moaned.

"Addison?" he prompted when she didn't answer. "Did you need me for something?"

She blinked in confusion, trying to remember what she'd come to his room for. He was going to think she was an idiot. "I...um...I came to tell you that we need to leave for the studio in..." She glanced down at her watch and was startled to see that they were already running late. "Oh no! We were supposed to leave ten minutes ago. The limo is probably already waiting for us. We'd better go."

Addison didn't give him a chance to reply, but turned and hurried out of the room.

As she had predicted, the limo was waiting for them in front of the house. Bob was talking to the driver, and both men turned in their direction as she and Trevor stepped outside.

Bob sat in front with the driver, whom he introduced as Leo, leaving Addison and Trevor alone in the back. As she settled into the seat, her slim skirt slid up her thighs, and she noticed Trevor's dark eyes caress her legs before he leaned forward to grab two bottles of Dasani Lemon from the bar.

He held one out to her. "Do you need a glass?"

She shook her head. "This is fine."

As she reached out to take the bottle, their fingers brushed, and it was all Addison could do not to squeal with delight. To stop herself from doing just that, she quickly unscrewed the cap and took a sip of the flavored water. To her embarrassment, some of it went the wrong way, and she ended up having a coughing fit.

Brow furrowing in concern, Trevor reached out to pat her on the back. "Are you sure you don't need a glass? Or maybe a straw?" he asked when she could finally talk.

Addison shook her head, totally embarrassed. "I'm fine. Really," she said. "I just drank too fast."

From the way Trevor was looking at her, she thought he might insist about the glass, but then he sat back in the seat beside her and took a swallow of water from his own bottle.

The rest of the drive was uneventful, much to Addison's relief. Though she was pleased Trevor had chosen to sit next to her, part of her would have preferred that he'd taken the seat across from her instead so she could have spent the drive looking at him. Even so, she still managed to steal several covert, sidelong glances without him knowing. Actors probably weren't used to their personal assistants fawning all over them, she reminded herself. She had to keep a rein on her inner-groupie.

When they arrived at the television studio a little while later, Addison was surprised to find security keeping a mob of screaming fan girls at bay outside the door. Trevor took it in stride, however, giving the women a wave and flashing that sexy grin of his as Bob escorted both of them into the studio.

Once inside, Addison was all set to wait in the green room with Trevor when she abruptly remembered Murray's instructions to talk to the show's producer about the kinds of questions that were off limits. Telling Trevor she would be right back, she hurried out of the room.

Finding the man took a little while and it wasn't until she finally tracked him down that she realized Murray had never told her what kinds of questions were off limits. Since she didn't know, she decided the best thing to do would be to ask the producer what the show host was going to talk to Trevor about.

"His new movie, mostly," the producer said. "And what other projects he has going on. That type of thing."

That sounded okay to Addison. Giving the man a smile, she thanked him for speaking with her, and then headed back to the green room. As she did so, she had the nagging suspicion that there was something else she was

18

supposed to do before the show, but for the life of her, she couldn't remember what it was. She really should have taken notes when Murray was rattling off his list of instructions.

Addison had always been glued to the television whenever Trevor was on, but she had to admit that it was a lot different in person. Not only were there all the cameras and lights, but there was the studio audience, too. Not surprisingly, it was almost all female.

She was so caught up in watching the clips from her boss's new movie that she didn't even notice the spotlight was shining directly into Trevor's eyes, forcing him to spend the whole interview leaning to one side in his chair. It was then that she remembered the other instruction Murray had given her. Crap, she was supposed to talk to the lighting guy. She was just making her way over to him when the show host announced that they were going to take a commercial break. She thought that would have made it easier to get the lighting guy's attention, but she'd barely finished speaking to him about the spotlight when the producer announced that they were back on the air.

Now that the spotlight wasn't shining directly into his eyes, Trevor looked a lot more relaxed, Addison noticed. Right up until the show host mentioned a rumor he'd heard about Trevor hooking up with some actress. Though Trevor tried to hide it, Addison saw from the way his jaw tightened that the question bothered him. Clearly that was one of those things that were supposed to have been off limits. Well, there was nothing she could do about it now.

On stage, Trevor smoothly turned the conversation back to his new movie, telling the show host that he'd have to wait and see whom he brought with him to the premiere. That seemed to satisfy the other man, who laughed.

Addison held her breath for the rest of the interview, half afraid the show host would ask something else he shouldn't, but to her relief, the man didn't bring up anything else controversial.

Bob met Addison and Trevor offstage, ready to escort them out to the limo. When they walked outside a few minutes later, however, the car was nowhere in sight. Her brow furrowing, she looked at her watch, wondering if they'd gotten done taping the show earlier than they were supposed to. But no, they were right on time.

Telling Trevor she would check on the limo, Addison dug into her shoulder bag for her cell phone and flipped it open, then thumbed through the list for Leo's cell number. When she got hold of that limo driver, she was going to give him a piece of her mind. When she finally got him on the phone and very politely asked where he was, however, the man told her that he was waiting right where he had dropped them off. Addison opened her mouth to argue with him when something made her frown.

She covered the mouthpiece with her hand and looked at Bob. "Did we come out a different door?"

The bodyguard nodded. "Yeah. We always go in the front and come out the back. Otherwise the fans mob Trevor. Murray didn't tell you that?"

It was on the tip of tongue to say no he hadn't, but then Addison saw Trevor regarding her thoughtfully and she flushed. Had Murray said something about that? She honestly couldn't remember. Turning her attention back to the limo driver, she gave Leo their new location and hung up. The man was Trevor's regular driver, so shouldn't he have known where to pick them up?

Dropping her phone back into her bag, she lifted her gaze to find Trevor still regarding her with those beautiful dark eyes. "I'm sorry, Mr. Bradon..." she began, but the rest of what she'd been about to say was drowned out by the mob of screaming fans heading their way.

Addison stared at the stampeding women in wide-eyed amazement. For one wild moment, she thought they might actually trample her to get to Trevor. But Bob stepped in front of them, spreading his arms and ordering in a booming voice, "Stop right there, ladies!"

Clearly intimidated by his large frame, the women stopped in their tracks. Then as a group, they began to beg for autographs and pictures. Remembering that Murray had said not to let Trevor sign any, she was just about to say something when he stepped forward and told Bob that he didn't mind signing some while they waited for the limo to get there.

Addison bit her lip, wondering if she should dissuade Trevor from the idea, but quickly decided against it. Between not remembering to talk to the lighting guy and the confusion with the limo, she'd already messed up enough for her first day on the job. With that in mind, she stood off to the side and watched while Trevor furiously signed one autograph after another for his adoring fans. She wondered if she could get him to sign one for her. Of course, she'd have to say it was for someone else.

She was just about to check with Leo again when the sleek, black car pulled up. Sighing with relief, Addison walked over to Trevor and going up on tiptoe, put her lips near his ear and announced that the limo had finally arrived.

Trevor nodded, but getting away from his fans was easier said than done. There always seemed to be one more woman that wanted an autograph. Bob had to finally step in and practically drag Trevor away from the mob. Even as he allowed his bodyguard to urge him into the car, Trevor was still all smiles and waves. His fans squealed and waved back.

Once she and Trevor were seated in the back of the limo, Addison gave him a sheepish look. "I'm sorry about the mix-up with the limo."

"Don't worry about it," Trevor said.

Though his handsome face gave nothing away, there was no mistaking the brusqueness in his deep voice, and Addison flushed. Surely he wouldn't fire her over this, would he? It was her first day, after all. Shoulders slumping, she turned to stare out the window.

Neither of them spoke the rest of the way back to Beverly Hills. When they got to his house, Addison was surprised to find the producer and director already waiting for them. She glanced at her watch and was shocked to see that her mistake back at the television studio had completely thrown them off schedule.

"They've been waiting for almost an hour," Maribel whispered, throwing a nervous glance over her shoulder at the two men in the living room. "I was afraid they were going to leave, so I've been trying to appease them with hors d'oeuvres."

Trevor scowled. "I'll take care of it. Thank you, Maribel."

Addison gave the cook a grateful smile before hurrying after Trevor. God, she hoped this didn't cost him the part.

But Trevor was extremely good at smoothing any feathers that had been ruffled, and after a few minutes, both men were more interested in discussing their movie than they were in the fact that Trevor had been late.

As Addison listened to them talk, her gaze strayed to the array of hors d'oeuvres on the table. She hadn't eaten since lunch and the sight of all that shrimp, lobster, and caviar was making her mouth water. She was just wondering if it was acceptable for personal assistants to eat during a meeting with their boss's potential employers when it suddenly occurred to her that all of the hors d'oeuvres had been made with seafood. Oh crap. She was supposed to tell Maribel that the director had an aversion to anything with seafood in it.

Hoping Maribel hadn't already left for the night, Addison murmured something about checking her messages, and then hurried into the kitchen. Fortunately, the cook was still there. She quickly explained the situation to the other woman.

"Do you have anything else we could serve?" Addison asked.

Maribel shook her head. "I make all my hors d'oeuvres by hand."

Great. Addison chewed on her lower lip, trying to come up with an idea. "What about cheese and crackers?" she asked after a moment. "I know it's not as fancy, but at least it's not seafood."

Maribel was silent as she considered the suggestion, but then she nodded. "I do have some cheese," she said, moving over to the refrigerator. "There are crackers in the pantry. Top shelf on your right."

The pantry was more like a small food store, so Addison had her pick of crackers. They were all fancier than anything she'd ever bought for herself, so she chose two boxes at random, and then set the crackers out on a plate while Maribel sliced an equally fancy assortment of cheeses.

Ten minutes later, Addison was back in the living room with a huge plate of cheese and crackers in her hands. Trevor was going over some lines for the part he'd be playing, and it was all she could do not to stop in her tracks and listen to his sexy voice.

Careful not to interrupt, she set the plate of cheese and crackers down on the coffee table, and then sat down in the overstuffed chair. She'd never really given much thought to how an actor went about getting a part in a movie, but the whole thing was extremely fascinating. Not nearly as fascinating as Trevor, though. Hearing him read for the part of a no-nonsense cop was almost enough to make her swoon.

Somehow, she managed to control herself, but only because Trevor had finished going over the script and was now discussing set locations. Noticing that the director could use a refill on his coffee, Addison picked up the carafe and at his nod, began to pour some into the cup he was holding. As she did so, she made the mistake of glancing over at Trevor. The moment her eyes met his, she completely forgot what she was supposed to be doing. The next thing she knew, the director was letting out a howl of pain.

Addison jerked out of her trance to find that she'd spilled hot coffee all over the director's pants.

"What the hell is wrong with you?!" the man demanded, jumping to his feet.

Heat suffused her face. "Oh God, I'm so sorry!" She set the carafe down on the table and grabbed a handful of cocktail napkins. "Here, let me..."

But the director grabbed the napkins out of her hand. "I think you've done enough," he said, giving her a hard look as he wiped his sodden pants.

Addison felt her color deepen. "I..." she began, but he had already turned his attention on Trevor.

"We'll be in touch," he said stiffly.

Throwing the napkins down on the coffee table, the director pushed past Addison and stormed out of the room. The producer murmured something to Trevor that she didn't catch before he left, too. A moment later, she heard the front door slam.

Addison gave Trevor a sheepish look. "I'm sorry. I wasn't paying attention, I guess, and..." the words trailed off at the dark look on his face. "I-I'll go and apologize."

She turned and would have hurried to the door, but Trevor caught her arm.

"I don't think that's a good idea," he told her. "Like Clive said, you've done enough damage already. I'll go."

24

Addison's bottom lip trembled as she watched Trevor walk out of the living room. If her carelessness had cost him this movie, then she was done for, she was sure of it.

Blinking back tears, Addison picked up two of the plates of uneaten hors d'oeuvres and carried them into the kitchen. Maribel frowned at the cheese and crackers.

"They didn't like that, either?" she asked.

Apparently, Maribel mustn't have heard the shouting, Addison thought as she set the plates down on the granite countertop. "They...um...had to leave."

The other woman's frowned deepened at that, but Addison didn't offer any more details. It was bad enough that she'd embarrassed herself in front of Trevor and his guests. Going back out into the living room, she collected the rest of the plates and carried them into the kitchen. Maribel was already covering the cheese and crackers with plastic wrap, and Addison grabbed one of the crab puffs before the women could do the same to the other hors d'oeuvres.

She was just working on her second one when Trevor walked in. From the look on his face, Addison couldn't tell if his talk with the director had gone well or not, and she braced herself.

"When you're finished here, I'd like to speak to you, Addison," he said. "I'll wait for you in your office."

Addison swallowed hard, the piece of crab puff almost getting caught in her throat. Well, at least he hadn't fired her in front of Maribel. Avoiding the other woman's curious gaze, she slid off the stool she'd been sitting on and left the kitchen.

She made her way down the hallway on leaden feet. She'd never gotten fired from any job she'd ever had, and the prospect of being given her walking papers after half a day as Trevor Braden's personal assistant made tears sting her eyes. If her sister found out, she'd never live it down.

Addison stood outside the door to her office for a moment to collect herself. Finally taking a deep breath, she walked in.

Trevor was leaning back against the desk, his arms folded across his broad chest, and Addison's pulse quickened. Even on the verge of being fired, all she could think about was how incredibly sexy he was.

"You wanted to see me?" she asked in a small voice.

He pushed away from the desk. "Close the door, if you would," he said.

Addison did as he asked, and then turned to face him. She waited for him to say something, but he only stood regarding her with those soulful dark eyes, his arms still crossed over his chest.

"Y-you're going to fire me, aren't you?" she asked, looking up at him from beneath lowered lashes.

"No," he said.

She blinked, not sure that she'd heard right. "You're not?"

"No," he said again. "But I am going to make sure that we don't have a repeat performance of what happened tonight."

Addison frowned, not sure where he was going with that. "I don't understand."

"Which is why I intend to make myself perfectly clear," he said.

As he spoke, Trevor took her arm and marched her over to the leather couch that was set along one wall. What was he going to do, sit her down and lecture her? She was just about to say that wouldn't be necessary when he sat down and pulled her unceremoniously over his knee.

Addison was so startled that for a moment all she could do was lay there draped over his muscular legs and stare down at the plush, beige carpet. What the heck was he doing? She craned her neck to look over her shoulder at him and was shocked to feel a sharp smack on her upturned bottom.

"Mr. Bradon, what...?" she gasped, only to let out a yelp as his hand came down again, this time on her other cheek. Oh my God, he was spanking her! "Trevor, what are you doing?!"

"I told you," he said, smacking her again. "I'm making sure that we don't have a repeat performance of tonight."

She yelped as his hand connected with her ass again. "By s-spanking me?!"

He met her gaze, his hand resting on the curve of her bottom. "It's the best way I can think of make sure you take your job seriously."

"I do take it seriously," she protested.

He lifted a brow. "Is that why you forgot to talk to the lighting guy? Or inform the show producer that personal questions were off limits? Or tell Leo to pick us up in back of the television studio? Or spilled coffee all over the director?"

After each question, he delivered several spanks to her upturned bottom, which was quickly beginning to sting.

Addison couldn't believe they were having this conversation while she was draped over his lap. Could anything be more embarrassing? "It's not like I did any of that on purpose! I honestly didn't know about the limo thing. And I only spilled the coffee because I..." Was looking at you. Her voice trailed off as she realized what she'd been about to say.

"Because you what, Addison?" he prompted.

She chewed on her lower lip, hesitating for a moment. "B-because I wasn't paying attention," she finally stammered.

"Then a spanking will help you to focus more," he said.

Before Addison could reply, he lifted his hand and began to smack her ass even harder. He worked back and forth, moving from one cheek to the other with an easy rhythm that made her wonder just how many women he'd spanked. While he wasn't spanking her as hard as he probably could have, the spanks still stung, and she let out a little yelp each time his hand connected with her bottom. Trevor, however, paid no attention to her protests, but simply held her down with a firm hand on her back as he continued to spank her.

She didn't know what was burning more, her face or her bottom. No matter how much she squirmed, she couldn't get away from his hand. But the embarrassment was even worse than the spanking. How could she possible look him in the eye after he had spanked her?

But then, just as quickly as it had begun, the spanking was over and she was back on her feet. Unable to help herself, Addison reached back with both hands to cup her tingling bottom.

Trevor reached out to gently lift her chin with his finger, forcing her to meet his gaze. "After that, I trust you'll pay more attention to your job."

All Addison could do was nod. When Trevor continued to just look at her, she wondered if he expected her to actually answer. But apparently, her nod must have been good enough because without another word, he turned and headed for the door.

Addison stared at his retreating back, still unable to believe that Trevor Bradon had actually put her over his knee and spanked her like a child. She should go up to her room, grab her bags, and leave, she told herself. But instead, she stood there rubbing her stinging bottom.

Chapter Two

Trevor lay in bed the next morning, staring up at the ceiling. What the hell had he been thinking last night? What bout of insanity had made him think that spanking his new personal assistant was a good idea? Could it be the number of times she had screwed up her first day on the job? God knew, she had certainly done enough of that. But that wasn't the reason he had put her over his knee. No, he had spanked Addison for one simple reason. He was absolutely mesmerized by her ass, plain and simple.

He had never really thought of himself as an assman, but the moment Addison had walked past him coming into the house yesterday, his eyes had been drawn to her bottom. Even concealed by the simple skirt she had been wearing, he could tell that it was perfect. Firm, but rounded, it had the most amazing wiggle when she walked. When she moved, he had automatically found himself following behind her the whole day, just to get a look at it.

Of course, the rest of her was equally alluring, from her beautiful face and long, blond hair to her lean, shapely legs and beautifully rounded breasts. But damn, that ass of hers was gorgeous!

When he had called her into her office to scold her last night for her less than stellar performance, he really had only intended to give her a reprimand. But then he'd caught a glimpse of her ass when she had turned to close the door and he'd suddenly been reminded of this movie he had done years ago. From that point on, it was like another part of him had taken over. He had just been along for the ride.

In the film, his saucy costar had been giving him grief. His character, a no-nonsense cop had responded by threatening to give the girl a good, sound spanking. Of course, the scene hadn't gone any further than that in the movie. But last night, it just seemed as if the situation had been begging for him to finally play it out. Which was exactly what he'd done. One second, he had been talking to Addison, and the next thing he knew, she'd been over his lap. He had never spanked a woman in his life before last night, but once he had Addison over his knee, it had come naturally.

And it had been amazing. Her ass had been just as tight as he'd imagined, and watching her wiggle that perfect bottom of hers while he'd brought his hand down on her cheeks again and again had to be the sexiest thing he'd ever seen. He had been hard as a rock for half the night, dreaming about how delectable she had looked.

But that had been last night, in the midst of some fit of madness. Now, in the clear and alarming light of day, he realized how incredibly stupid he had been.

Oh yeah, he was going to pay big for those few moments of insanity. He could see the tabloid headlines now.

HOLLYWOOD HUNK PADDLES ASSISTANT!

Access Hollywood would probably run a special segment on him, maybe Entertainment Tonight, too. They'd call it "Hollywood Men and the Women They Spank." Damn, this was going to be bad.

Trevor ran a hand through his hair. Maybe he could smooth things over with Addison by apologizing to her, he thought. He could promise not to spank her again. Even offer her a pay raise. He swore under his breath. Who the hell was he kidding? He was screwed. He might as well go downstairs and face the firing squad. Hell, for all he knew, Addison had left in the middle of the night and was already telling her story to some slimy reporter. He could only hope that Murray was as good at damage control as he was at managing money.

With a groan, Trevor rolled out of bed and headed for the adjoining bathroom. He needed a shower. And yet even though he knew he was going to be in for one hell of a long day, he still found himself thinking about Addison Mattingly and that gorgeous ass of hers.

* * *

Addison still wasn't sure why she hadn't gone upstairs, packed her bags, and left after Trevor had spanked her last night. It would have been the smart thing to do really. But instead she had calmly gone up to her bedroom and unpacked, as if getting spanked on the first day of the job was the most natural thing in the world. For all she knew, maybe in Hollywood, it was.

Lying in bed now, she could almost believe that she had imagined the whole thing. But as she replayed the entire embarrassing scene over in her head, she knew that she hadn't. Trevor had put her over his knee and spanked her. She should be furious with him, she told herself. Oddly enough, though, she wasn't. She had screwed up a lot yesterday, and while that certainly didn't justify him given her a spanking, it did explain his actions. Besides, it hadn't really hurt. Nothing besides her pride, that was. Did she really want to walk away from her dream job over a little spanking? But how the heck could she look him in the eye after last night?

She sighed. While part of her wanted to leave, the other part of her – the part that had made her come to LA and take the job as Trevor Braden's personal assistant in the first place – wanted to stay. That was the part she ended up listening to.

Telling herself it wouldn't look good to be late her second day on the job, Addison got out of bed and padded into the adjoining bathroom. Taking a quick shower, she put on her make-up, pulled her long hair back in a loose bun, then got dressed. Hoping the simple black skirt and light blue blouse looked professional enough, she slipped her feet into a pair of black pumps and left the room.

Knowing she should probably go to her office first, but unable to resist the delicious smell of food coming from the kitchen, Addison made her way there instead. Maribel was standing at the stove making pancakes, and she looked up as Addison walked in.

Maribel smiled. "Good morning. You're just in time for breakfast."

Addison looked longingly at the pancakes. "I'd love to, but I'm just going to grab some coffee and take it to my office."

The other woman's brow furrowed. "Nonsense! You need a good breakfast to start the day."

Addison couldn't help but smile at the motherly tone in the cook's voice. "Probably, but I slept later than I should have and I really need to get to work," she said, and then added, "After that debacle with the hors d'oeuvres last night, I don't want to give Trevor – Mr. Bradon, I mean – a reason to fire me."

Mabel waved her hand. "Good heavens! Trevor isn't going to fire you for having breakfast. Now, pour yourself a cup of coffee. The pancakes will be done in a few minutes."

Addison knew she should have protested, but the thought of having pancakes was already making her stomach growl. "Okay," she agreed, moving to get a mug from the cabinet. "But at least let me help with breakfast."

Though she wanted to help, Addison had never been particularly handy in the kitchen, so she was glad when the other woman didn't ask her to do anything more complicated than cut up some fresh fruit.

While Addison sliced the strawberries, Maribel told her about her family, and her newest granddaughter, in particular. Addison didn't come from a big family herself,

32

but had always thought it would be nice. She couldn't help but laugh as Maribel regaled her with one amusing story after the other. It really sounded like the woman had a great family. Of course, at some point Maribel got around to asking about Addison's family. Addison made sure she was very careful how she answered. She didn't want to slip up and mention her twin sister. That might lead to some awkward questions that she didn't want to answer.

"How long had you worked for Trevor?" Addison asked, changing the subject as she reached for another strawberry. "I mean, Mr. Braden," she quickly corrected herself when she'd realized that she had used his first name again.

Maribel laughed. "You can call him Trevor, honey. We all do around here," she said as she ladled more pancake batter on the griddle. "I've been with Trevor since he first started out in the business. Of course, he lived in a one-bedroom apartment back then, and all I did was make him meals and show up once a week to put them in the freezer." She smiled fondly at the memory. "It started out as a favor to his mother, really. She and I have been friends since we were little girls. She called me and told me that she was afraid Trevor would come down here to LA and forget to take good care of himself. You know, not eat right and so forth. So, since I lived nearby I said I'd look in on him and make him some healthy meals. Trevor insisted he pay me, but I wouldn't hear of it. The poor boy made a pittance back then. He could barely afford to pay the rent on his apartment, much less anything else." She slid the spatula underneath one of the pancakes and expertly flipped it over. "When he finally got a starring role in his own television show, he insisted on putting me on the payroll and wouldn't take no for answer. And you know what? It was the best decision I ever made."

Addison remembered the television show she was talking about. It was called LA Nights. Trevor had played a uniformed cop with the LAPD who had been pulled off the streets to go undercover in the nightclub scene. It was the first time she had ever seen Trevor, and she had fallen in love with him, along with every other girl on the planet. Little did she know then that her celebrity crush had a habit of putting his personal assistants over his knee and spanking them, she thought wryly. Not as many women might have been so crazy for him if they knew that.

Who the heck was she kidding? There were probably thousands of women out there that would fall all over themselves at the chance to lie over Trevor's lap for a spanking if it meant getting to be that close to him. Who knew? Maybe he spanked all his assistants.

For some reason, that thought bothered Addison and she found herself quizzing Maribel about Trevor's previous personal assistants. "How many has he had before me?" she asked. "And why did they leave?"

Maribel transferred two of the pancakes to a plate. "How many? There was only the one, Sophia. She started about the same time I did, I think. She was good at it, but the job just got to be too hard for her. She and her husband moved to Florida and enjoy their grandkids." The cook gave Addison a smile as she set the plate down in front of her. "She thought Trevor needed someone younger to keep up with him," she added, winking at her.

Addison felt herself blush, and she quickly busied herself with putting some sliced strawberries on her pancakes. It was nice to know that Trevor's previous assistant had left because she wanted to spend time with her grandchildren and not because of something he'd done. And for some perverse reason, it made Addison feel better knowing that Trevor probably hadn't spanked her, either, seeing as the woman was obviously old enough to be his mother.

She was just putting syrup on her pancakes when Trevor walked into the kitchen. His dark hair was damp from the shower and he was dressed in shorts and a T-shirt. It was all Addison could do not to stare. God, he was enough to make her mouth water!

Abruptly realizing she was in fact staring, Addison put down the pitcher of syrup. Lowering her gaze to look down at her plate, she was surprised to see that her pancakes were swimming in syrup. She had been so distracted by Trevor's gorgeous body that she hadn't been paying attention to what she'd been doing. Just like last night when she'd spilled coffee all over the director.

"There you are!" Maribel said to Trevor. "Sit down and I'll make you some pancakes."

When Trevor didn't answer, Addison looked up at him from beneath her long bangs to find him regarding her with those soulful brown eyes of his. She held her breath, waiting for him to say something, such as, "You're fired," but after a moment he turned his attention to Maribel.

"Thanks, but I want to work out before I head over to the studio," he said. "I'll grab something to eat later."

Addison waited for Maribel to give Trevor the same lecture she'd gotten about the importance of eating a good breakfast, but he left the kitchen before the woman could even open her mouth. Addison chewed on her lip as she watched him go. Was Trevor as uncomfortable about what had happened between them last night as she was? Addison wondered. If so, didn't that mean he wouldn't be as likely to put her over his knee and spank her again?

Relieved that she probably wouldn't be getting any more spankings, Addison picked up her fork. Even with all the syrup she had put on them, the pancakes were delicious. Thanking Maribel for breakfast after she was done, Addison picked up her coffee and went to her office.

Remembering reading something on the schedule about doing a few pick-up shots for the movie he'd just finished filming, Addison picked up the day-planner from her desk and flipped through it. Finding the contact number for the studio in the book Murray had given her, Addison called and introduced herself, then checked to make sure she knew exactly where Trevor had to be and when he had to be there. Hanging up the phone, she thumbed through the book looking for Leo's number, but then decided it would be easier to simply go see him instead.

The tall, blond driver was in the garage stocking the fridge in the limo with bottled water, and he looked up when she walked in.

"Hey," he said, giving her a grin as he climbed out of the car. "Good to see we didn't chase you off. What can I do for you?"

She smiled. "I just wanted to remind you that Trevor has to be at the studio at ten o'clock."

Leo nodded. "Got ya. I'll have the car out front at nine then."

"Thanks," she said and was about to go back inside when Leo stopped her.

"Hang on a minute, Addison."

She turned back to see him heading over to a small office on the other side of the garage. Ducking inside, he grabbed something from the desk, then jogged back over to hand her a small walkie-talkie.

"So you can get hold of me easier if you and Trevor come out a different door again," he told her with a grin. "Ever use one of these before?"

She shook her head.

"It's easy. Just press this button and hold it down to talk, then release it so that I can talk to you," he said, pointing to a rectangular-shaped button on the side of the radio. "It's good within about a mile or so. Just ignore all these other buttons. It has a lot of other capabilities, but we don't need to worry about those right now."

She smiled. "Thanks. I really appreciate this."

He grinned. "No problem."

Radio in hand, Addison went back inside the house. Rather than go back to her office right away, though, she found herself heading to the gym instead. While she told herself it was just so she could make sure Trevor knew what time they needed to leave, she had to admit that she wouldn't mind watching him work out.

When she walked in the gym a few moments later, Trevor was lifting weights. He had taken off his T-shirt and was sitting on a padded bench, legs spread, one arm on his muscular thigh while he worked out his biceps. Addison's pulse quickened at the sight of him. She watched breathlessly as his muscles flexed and rippled. Damn, he looked fine all hot and sweaty. It was all she could do not to walk over to him and run her hands over him.

Stifling a moan, Addison cleared her throat and walked into the room. "Mr. Braden."

At the sound of his name, Trevor looked up. He didn't stop what he was doing, though, and Addison had to force her gaze away from the muscles flexing in his broad chest.

"I...um...just wanted to remind you that we have to leave for the studio in a little while," she said.

He nodded. "Thanks. I'm almost done here."

She chewed on her lower lip, watching the muscles in his arm bulge as he lifted the weight. "I'll see you out front then."

Addison made as if to go, but the sound of her name had her turning back around to face Trevor. He had set the weight done and gotten to his feet. A bead of sweat slowly ran down his chest, and she stared at it as if mesmerized.

"I...um..." Trevor began, then stopped and ran a hand through his hair.

Her heart lurched. Oh God, he was going to mention the spanking he'd given her.

But to her relief, he didn't. "Do you think you could pick out something for me to wear while I take a shower?" he asked. "Anything is fine. I'll be changing when I get to the studio anyway."

"Oh," she said. "Yeah. Of course."

"Thanks," he said, flashing her a grin as he grabbed his shirt from the weight bench.

Though she was relieved that Trevor hadn't brought up the spanking, Addison had to admit that she wouldn't have minded if he had apologized for putting her over his knee. It was the least he could do, she thought as she made her way upstairs.

* * *

Trevor stole a glance at Addison as they drove to the studio later that morning. She hadn't said a word to him since they'd left the house thirty minutes earlier, but had instead spent the time reading through her day-planner and making notes in the margins. He didn't know what to make of her silence. He had been stunned to walk into the kitchen and find her sitting there. He had immediately steeled himself for a confrontation regarding his inappropriate behavior the night before, but she hadn't given any indication that anything had happened at all. She had just calmly poured syrup on her pancakes. Realizing that she wouldn't want to discuss what had happened in front of Maribel, he had made a point of saying he was going to the gym, thinking she would follow. But she hadn't come in until nearly an hour later, and then it was only to remind him about going to the studio. He had almost brought up the spanking himself, but then decided against it, asking her to pick out something for him to wear instead. He figured that since she hadn't brought it up, then maybe he shouldn't, either.

Looking at her now, he wondered again if he should apologize for spanking her, but then thought better of it. Maybe Addison had simply decided to forget about the whole thing. God, he hoped so. Putting her over his knee had been the dumbest thing he had ever done, and he promised himself right then and there that he wasn't going to do it again.

Relieved that he wouldn't have to worry about last night's spanking showing up in the tabloids, Trevor leaned back in his seat and went over his lines. He was just doing a few pick-up shots for the movie he'd recently finished filming. They had to do that sometimes, when the sound on the original set was horrible or when something didn't look as good on film as they thought it would. When that happened, they would build a lookalike for the original set back on a sound stage, and redo the scene there. The scene was an easy one, so it should only take an hour, two at the most. That was good. He looked forward to getting home and relaxing. The staff only worked half a day on Wednesdays, which meant that he would have the place to himself. It had been a while since he'd just spent the day hanging out and doing nothing. Maybe he would do some laps in the pool.

When they arrived at the studio, Trevor let Addison step out of the limo first. As she did so, he found his gaze automatically going to her bottom. Damn, damn, and double damn. She had an amazing ass! Thoughts of her wiggling around on his lap while he spanked her came to mind unbidden, and he let out a groan as he felt his cock go hard inside his jeans. Down boy, he told himself. Under no circumstances was he ever going to put his personal assistant over his knee and spank her again.

Two hours later, however, he was beginning to think that maybe he shouldn't have made such a silly promise. If there were ever a girl who needed her bottom warmed again, it was Addison.

Everything had gone fine at first. He had introduced Addison to everyone, and then the director's assistant had shown her around while he and the director went over the details of the shoot with the stunt coordinator and the other actors. In today's pick-up shots, Trevor was doing a scene in which he was tied to a chair in a dirty basement while some hired thugs worked him over to extract some secret info. He had worked with the stunt guys a dozen times before and they knew their business. They would lay into him with some great looking fake punches. All he had to do was react to their near misses, spit out the fake blood on cue, and of course, spout the usual manly one-liners. It was a piece of cake. Or it would have been if it hadn't been for Addison.

She was sitting with the rest of the film crew, off to one side, which would have been okay if she hadn't forgotten about the whole quiet-on-the-set rule. When Trevor refused to answer one of the thug's questions and the stunt guy playing the part drew back his fist and faked a nice blow right across his jaw, Addison must have thought it was real because she gasped and let out a loud, "Oh!"

"Cut!" the director yelled, then looked around, an annoyed look on his face. "What the hell was that?"

Trevor turned his head to look at Addison, as did everyone else.

She blushed and gave them a sheepish look. "Sorry," she said. "It just looked so real. It won't happen again."

But it did. Over and over and over again. Every time the stunt guys hit him, she either gasped, groaned, squealed, or jumped so high that her chair rattled. When he finally undid the ropes and broke loose to land a roundhouse kick in the stunt guy's stomach, she actually cheered like it was the real thing. Which meant that they had to redo the whole scene over again.

By the time they had finally finished – five hours later - Trevor was exhausted and his jaw hurt. A couple of times the stunt guys' "fake" punches had landed for real. Not that he supposed he could really blame the men. Addison's had them so frustrated, he was surprised that they hadn't beaten the crap out of him. She did work for him, after all.

Addison didn't say much in the limo on the way back to the house, other than to apologize again for being such a distraction at the shoot. "It just all looked so real," she said.

Trevor ground his jaw. If she'd only done it once or twice, then he might be more understanding, but after five hours and twenty-five takes, he wasn't feeling all that gracious. If it weren't for Bob and Leo sitting in the front seat, he would have put Addison over his knee and tanned her bottom right there in the limo. But then he reminded himself about his promise. No, he would not spank her.

When they got back to the house, Bob asked Trevor if he needed anything before he took off, but Trevor shook his head.

Once inside, Addison walked into living room. "I'm starving. I'm going to see if Maribel has anything to snack on before dinner."

"Maribel isn't here," he said.

Addison's brow furrowed. "She isn't?"

"The staff only works half a day on Wednesday. That includes Leo and Bob," he told her. "But thanks to you, they had to spend the day hanging around the studio waiting for me to finish those pick-up shots."

Her face colored. "I said I was sorry."

He lifted a brow. "Just like you were sorry for spilling coffee on the director last night, right?"

She lifted her chin, her blue eyes flashing. "It wasn't like I messed up your stupid pick-up shots deliberately, you know."

Stupid pick-up shots? Trevor's mouth tightened. "Those stupid pick-up shots are what pays your salary," he said, then shook his head. "I promised myself I wouldn't do this again, but it's obvious that the only way I'm going to get through to you is with another spanking."

Addison's eyes went wide at the mention of a spanking, but before she could say anything, Trevor took her arm and led her over to the couch. She tried to hang back, but one tug had her over his knee the moment he sat down.

She tried to push herself off his lap, but a hand on the small of her back held her firmly in place. "Let me up right now!" she demanded.

"I don't think so," Trevor said. "I'm thinking that I didn't spank you enough last night, so this time, I'm not letting you up until I'm sure I'm getting through to you."

She lifted her head to look over her shoulder at him. "You can't do this to me! It's wrong!"

Trevor didn't answer right away, but instead brought his hand down on her upturned bottom. Two quick smacks, one on each cheek. "What's wrong is you making a complete mess of what should have been a very simple film shoot."

She started to reply, but then gasped when he delivered several more smacks to each cheek.

"Owwww!" she squealed. "That's too hard!"

He snorted. "Oh please," he said. "I'm not spanking you any harder than you deserve. And not nearly as hard as I'm going to be spanking you before I'm done."

Even he was surprised by the tone of his voice. When the hell had he become this authoritative? he wondered. Maybe it was Addison. She seemed to have a way of bringing it out in him. He'd never met any woman who could get under his skin like she could. As he lifted his hand and brought it down sharply on her upturned

42

bottom again, he knew he probably shouldn't be doing this. But he couldn't seem to stop himself.

Addison was kicking her legs and yelping after each smack to her delicious ass. The way she was moving was really getting to him. His cock was already hard as a rock where it pressed against hip. Thank God she was obviously too preoccupied with the spanking to notice how turned on he was.

He took his time, working back and forth from one cheek to the other, making sure he didn't bring his hand down on the same spot twice. She might deserve this spanking, but he certainly didn't want to really hurt her. He just wanted her bottom to sting enough so that she would remember this the next time she was tempted to do something she shouldn't.

As he watched her ass wiggle under her tight skirt, Trevor had an almost uncontrollable urge to grab the hem of it and pull it up. God, he bet her ass was beautiful. Probably even more so now that it was a nice shade of pink.

But he resisted the urge. That would definitely be going way too far. He would just have to content himself with spanking her until her bottom glowed under that skirt.

"Okay, okay!" she squealed. "You've made your point! I won't interrupt any more film shoots. I promise."

Trevor delivered a few more smacks as he thought about her promise. While he would have enjoyed spanking her for hours, he knew her bottom couldn't take that. It was probably stinging pretty good already. Besides, she was right; he had made his point.

With one harder smack on the ass, he took Addison's hand and helped her to her feet. She didn't look at him as she reached back to cup her freshly-spanked bottom. Getting to his feet, he reached out to lift her chin with a finger. She glared up at him defiantly as she rubbed her ass. God, did she even know how sexy that was?

"No more mistakes," he warned her. "I don't want to have to spank you again, but I will if I have to. Do you understand?"

She nodded. "Yes."

She might have said yes, but her eyes still flashed with spirit. A little spanking like this wasn't going to tame her. "Good," he said, though he wasn't sure if he was referring to her answer or to her spunk.

Without another word, she turned and left the room. As she did so, Trevor's gaze remain fixed on her ass the whole time. Damn, he was starting to wish he had pulled up that skirt.

* * *

Up in her room, Addison went directly over to the closet and took out her suitcases and unzipped them. Marching over to the dresser, she yanked open the top drawer, took out her neatly folded stacks of bikini panties and threw them in one of the bags. Two spankings in two days. And all because she got a little carried away while watching Trevor film a movie. It was too much. She was leaving!

She blinked back tears as she opened another drawer. She was a complete and utter failure as a personal assistant. Worse, she had making a complete fool of herself in front of her favorite actor. But she had been so worried for Trevor when those stunt men had been beating him up. It had looked so real. She just hadn't been able to control her reaction. And Trevor had spanked her for it. She reached back with one hand to rub her tender bottom. There probably wasn't another personal assistant in all of Hollywood who got spanked by their boss.

Addison threw the rest of her stuff in the suitcases, and then went into the bathroom to collect her toiletries. Zipping her bags closed, she picked them up and walked out of the room and into the hallway. She stopped on the landing, however, as angry voices drifted up from downstairs.

Her brow furrowed as she recognized Murray's voice. "It's her fault you didn't get the role in that movie! I don't know why the hell I ever hired her"

Addison chewed on her lower lip. Murray had obviously heard about her spilling coffee on the director last night and blamed her for Trevor not getting the movie role. Her heart sunk even lower. She wouldn't have to quit, she was about to get fired.

"Lay off her, Murray," Trevor said. "The director wasn't sold on me even before Addison spilled coffee on him. Besides, I thought the guy was a jerk. Addison just did what I was thinking about doing."

Addison blinked, surprised that Trevor had defended her. She quietly set down her suitcases and moved closer to the top of the stairs so that she could see into the living room. Trevor and Murray were standing face to face in the middle of the room. Trevor looked calm, but Murray looked totally apoplectic.

"That's bullshit!" Murray spat. "Is that twit in her office? I'm going to fire her right now!"

Murray didn't wait for a reply. Instead, he headed for the hallway that led to the back of the house and her office. Trevor's voice halted the man before he could take more than two steps.

"No, Murray, you aren't," he said.

Murray turned to look at Trevor. "Why the hell not?"

Addison held her breath as she waited for Trevor to answer.

"Because the job comes with a learning curve and she's doing fine," he said.

Murray stared at him in disbelief. "She's a disaster, Trevor. She needs to go!"

He turned to leave again, probably to go to her office, Addison thought, but again, Trevor's deep voice halted him.

"I said she stays, Murray."

Murray's eyes narrowed, and for a moment, Addison thought that he was going to press the issue, but instead, he just shook his head.

"Fine!" he snapped. "Have it your way. But another screw-up and she's out of here!"

Turning on his heel, he stormed out of the room. A moment later, Addison heard the front door slam. Oh my God, she couldn't believe it. Trevor had not only defended her, but had made sure she kept her job. Why would he do that? After the way she'd messed up, she would have thought he'd be happy to see her go.

"What's his problem?" Bob asked, walking into the living room.

Trevor ran his hand through his hair. "He's just pissed I didn't get the part in that new movie."

Bob snorted. "Forget about him. He's an asshole."

Trevor made no comment, so Addison supposed that meant he agreed with the bodyguard's assessment of Murray.

"I thought you were going to the gym to work out," Trevor said, changing the subject.

"I am," Bob said. "How 'bout you come along and spot for me?"

"Yeah, why not," Trevor said. "I'll go change and meet you in the gym."

Abruptly realizing that Trevor was starting for the stairs, Addison grabbed her suitcases off the floor and hurried back to her room, quietly closing the door behind her. Ten minutes ago, she had been determined to quit her job and walk out on Trevor, but after the way he had defended her to Murray, she couldn't leave.

With a sigh, she unzipped her suitcases and began to unpack.

Chapter Three

Addison woke up early the next morning, eager to put the past two days behind her and start fresh. Trevor had an interview and a photo shoot for a magazine scheduled for noon that day and she was determined to make sure everything went right. She was going to be the best damn personal assistant an actor ever had. And she was not going to do anything to earn herself another spanking!

Blushing at the thought, she pushed back the blanket, then got out of bed and went into the bathroom to take a quick shower. When she was done, she put on her make-up, pulled her long hair up in a loose bun, then slipped into a simple navy blue wrap-dress and a pair of high-heeled sandals. After checking her appearance in the full-length mirror, she left her room and went downstairs.

When she walked into the kitchen a few minutes later, Maribel greeted her with a warm smile.

"I was just about to make breakfast?" Maribel opened the fridge and took out a carton of eggs. "How does an omelet sound? And don't tell me you're just going to grab some coffee and take it to your office."

Addison smiled. She actually hadn't even considered it. Maribel's cooking was too good to pass up. Although if Addison ate pancakes and omelets every morning, she wasn't going to be able to fit through the door to get into her office!

"Can you make mine an egg-white omelet instead?" she asked.

"I sure can. I'll put in some tomatoes and herbs, too." Maribel winked at her. "Give those egg whites some more flavor."

Addison laughed. Walking over to one of the cabinets, she took out a mug, then poured herself some coffee. As she added cream and sugar, she glanced at Maribel. "Do you know if Trevor is up yet?"

She tried to make the question sound as casual as she could, but the smile that curved Maribel's lips was all too knowing, and Addison hastily sipped her coffee to hide the blush that rose to her cheeks.

"He's up and already been out for a jog," the older woman said. "He's showering, I think."

An image of water pouring down Trevor's naked body while he ran his soap-covered hands over his muscular chest and rock-hard abs had Addison's pulse skipping a beat. Her face colored even more. Thankfully, Maribel already had turned back to the stove so she didn't see.

Setting her mug down, Addison walked over to the fridge. Taking out the loaf of whole wheat bread, she put a slice in the outrageously high-tech stainless-steel toaster on top of the granite countertop.

"Put a couple slices in for Trevor, too," Maribel said, glancing up from the stove. "He should be down any minute."

Addison did as the other woman asked, but didn't toast them right away since she had no idea when Trevor was going to come downstairs. While she waited for her own slice of bread to toast, she watched as Maribel expertly made breakfast. Not a cook by any stretch of the imagination, Addison was amazed by how easy the omelet slid out of the pan and onto the plate. If she'd tried that, it would have stuck for sure. It looked so light and fluffy, too. How did Maribel do that?

Eager to see if the egg, tomato, and herb combination tasted as fantastic as it looked, Addison picked up her fork and was about to dig in when Trevor walked into the kitchen. She stared at him, the omelet in front of her completely forgotten. He was wearing jeans and a T-shirt, his hair still damp from the shower and his feet thrust into a pair of leather flip-flops. He looked laid-back and absolutely gorgeous.

He flashed her a smile. "Morning."

Addison knew she should return the greeting, but she was so caught up in the man himself, she couldn't seem to get the words out. She decided it would be easier to give him a smile instead.

"I'll make you an omelet," Maribel said. "Sit down."

Addison told herself she should eat before her own eggs got cold, but she didn't think it would be polite, so she sipped her coffee while she waited for Maribel to make Trevor's omelet.

There were several stools at the breakfast bar and Addison was surprised and also a little bit giddy when Trevor sat down in the one beside her after he'd poured himself some coffee. His nearness made her pulse do all sorts of crazy things and she had to remind herself not to gaze at him like a lovestruck fangirl.

Trevor glanced at her as he took a swallow of coffee. "Did you sleep okay?"

Addison nodded. "Yes, thanks." Suddenly self-conscious, she fingered the handle on her coffee mug. "I was checking your calendar and you have an interview for Men's Fitness at noon today, followed by a photo shoot."

He groaned. "Oh hell, I forgot. That's as much fun as getting a root canal."

She looked at him in surprise. "Should I cancel it?"

He shook his head. "Nah. I don't mind the interview so much. It's the photo shoot part I hate."

Her brow furrowed. "Really? Why? I would think it'd be fun."

Trevor took another swallow of coffee. "It probably would be if I didn't have to stand in the hot sun

50

for hours while some arty photographer tells me to smile but look dangerous at the same time. I might be an actor, but I have no idea how to do both at the same time."

Addison laughed. "Well, I'll be there, so I can translate if you want."

His mouth twitched. "As long as you don't do what you did during the pick-up shots yesterday."

She blushed at the reminder, particularly since it conjured up images of the spanking she'd gotten for her misdeeds.

"What happened yesterday?" Maribel asked as she set Trevor's omelet down in front of him.

He picked up the salt shaker and sprinkled some on his eggs, then did the same with the pepper. "Addison got a little carried away watching the fight scene and ended up interrupting every five minutes. She forgot we were acting."

Addison gave the other woman a sheepish look. "It all looked so real. I thought those guys were actually beating Trevor up."

"You thought who was beating Trevor up?"

Addison turned to see Bob coming into the kitchen. He looked curiously from Trevor to her, then back again.

"Addison thought the stunt men I was doing the fight scene with were really beating me up in the pick-up shots I did yesterday," Trevor explained. "Every time they took a swing at me, she gasped and we had to keep reshooting the scene over and over."

Bob chuckled. "So that's why you too so long." He looked away from Trevor to give Addison a wink. "I thought you kept forgetting your lines or something."

Trevor's mouth twitched. "Very funny. It's not hard to remember your lines when all you have to do is grunt and gasp."

Bob and Maribel laughed. So did Addison. Trevor joined in and after that, the entire story came out as he told them about how she had reacted during yesterday's filming. Looking back on the whole thing, Addison had to admit it was kind of funny. Right up until the spanking, of course, but even that didn't seem like such a big deal now. Trevor obviously wasn't that concerned about it.

After breakfast, Trevor announced he was going to go lift some weights before they left so he'd be pumped for the photo shoot. Addison ran her gaze appreciatively over his biceps. She didn't think that'd be a problem.

Trevor glanced at her as he got to his feet. "While I'm doing that, maybe you could take care of some online financial stuff for me? I was going to do it myself, but I'd rather just work out."

She's much rather watch him pump iron, but didn't say so. Instead, she nodded and slipped off the stool, taking her coffee mug with her. "Sure."

"Murray usually does most of it," Trevor explained as they walked down the hall to her office. "But I like to handle some of the bills myself."

Addison was a little surprised Trevor trusted her enough to handle his money, especially after all the screw-ups. It made her feel good to know he had so much confidence in her. Then again, maybe he figured if she didn't do the bills right, he'd just spank her again.

Embarrassed at the thought, Addison hastily sat down at her desk and turned on her computer, then connected to the internet. Trevor came around the desk to stand beside her chair and leaned over to type in the bank's website address. His bare arm brushed up against hers, sending a little shiver of pleasure through her body, and she caught her breath. Concentrating on anything was going to be difficult with him so close, she decided, and was relieved when he wrote down his account numbers and access codes on a piece of paper for her instead, then did the same with the list of payees and amounts he wanted her to pay.

Addison used the same bank, so she was used to paying bills online, which should make paying Trevor's bills a snap. Of course, he had a lot more accounts with a lot more money in them. She tried not to let her eyes bulge as she took in the amounts.

"What about these?" she asked, pointing at several accounts at the bottom of the screen. She hoped he wouldn't think she was being nosy by asking, but she didn't want to accidently take money from the wrong account.

Trevor didn't seem to mind, though. "Those are direct links to some investment groups Murray has my money in. It's embarrassing to admit, but I really don't pay that much attention to them. Murray just shows me the portfolio numbers every once in a while. They're something to do with real estate, I think." He gave her a sheepish look. "That sounds kind of pathetic, doesn't it?"

She shook her head. "No, not at all. That's why you have good people around you to take care of things like that so you can focus on your acting."

The corner of his mouth edged up. "That's the way I figure it, too. Speaking of focusing, I'd better get to the gym. Give me about and hour and I'll be buff, showered-off, and ready to go. Thanks again for the help and if you run into any problems, just come get me."

Addison was so lost in images of Trevor getting all buffed-up and showered-off, she barely heard that last part. As he left the room, she found her gaze dipping to his jean-clad butt. Damn, he had a great ass.

Letting out a little sigh, Addison turned her attention back to the computer. There really weren't all that many bills to pay. Along with the utility bills, there was Trevor's cell phone bill and one for a personal credit card. She couldn't help but notice he carried a very low balance on his credit card. Considering the outrageous credit limit they were offering him, it was both surprising and reassuring to see he didn't just blow through his credit cards like some people in Hollywood were rumored to do. It made her like him even more than she already did.

Paying Trevor's bills reminded her that she hadn't paid her own before she'd left San Francisco. Since she wasn't sure how the job as Trevor's personal assistant would pan out, she hadn't bothered to get rid of her apartment, so she still had to keep paying both rent and utilities. She hadn't actually quit her previous job, either, but just taken some vacation days instead. She still had plenty of vacation time saved up, so she should be okay for a while. It would probably be a good idea to hold on to her other job for now in case she got fired from this one.

After paying the bills, she took a quick look at Trevor's investment accounts just out of curiosity. It wasn't snooping if she had permission, right?

One was with a New York investment firm that sounded really snooty and upper class. She'd never heard of it, of course. That wasn't surprising, though, considering her knowledge of investing ended with the two-hundred-and-fifty dollars she had in her savings. She got the feeling she probably couldn't open an account there with that measly amount of money.

The second was mutual fund that she recognized from their advertisements on television. If she remembered correctly, the minimum investment amount was ten-thousand dollars. Oh well, so much for that investment opportunity.

Lastly, there was something that looked like it could be the real estate investment Trevor had mentioned. He had a whole lot of his money in that one, way more than in the other two. Curious, she Googled the name Total Empire Investment Trust, then clicked on the link to their website.

The homepage was very prestigious, with an impressive looking building in the background and an investment board made up of men who had some really serious expressions on their faces. She browsed the site, wondering if maybe she should invest a little money in the company, too. Of course, from how high class their website was, she'd probably need a minimum investment of a million dollars or something equally outrageous. All the same, it wouldn't hurt to call and ask. She bookmarked the page. Maybe they would give her a discount since she worked for Trevor.

Addison had just finished up and was logging off when Bob stuck his head in her office.

"Got a minute?" he asked.

She smiled. "Sure, come on in. What did you need?" she asked as he sat down in one of the chairs in front of her desk.

"Nothing, really," he admitted. "I just wanted to see how things are going with the job."

She shrugged. "Not bad, I guess."

He frowned. "You don't like the work?"

"I love it," she admitted. "I'm just not very good at it."

"You mean that stuff you did during the pick-up shots yesterday?" At her nod, he continued. "You're being too hard on yourself. Being a personal assistant is a tough job. It took years for Sophia to get the hang of it and she still got it wrong more often than not. You're doing fine. Just give yourself a chance."

She sighed. "I'm more concerned about Trevor giving me a chance."

"Don't worry about that. Trevor likes you."

Addison blinked in surprise. "You think so?"

Bob grinned. "Hell yeah. I haven't heard him laugh like he did this morning in a long time. You're good for him."

Just because Bob thought so, that didn't mean Trevor would agree, but the words pleased her anyway. "Well, let's just hope I don't do anything stupid at the photo shoot." She glanced at her watch. "Speaking of which, I'd better go see if Trevor's ready to leave."

"Sounds good," Bob said. "I'll have Leo bring the car around."

Trevor had already finished working out and was just coming down from upstairs when Addison walked into the living room a few minutes later. Dressed in jeans and a fresh tee, he looked just as buff as he promised.

"Any problems with the bills?" he asked as they stepped into the foyer.

She shook her head. "No. I paid all of them."

He nodded and opened the door for her. "So, where are the interview and photo shoot anyway?"

Addison flipped open her day-planner to that day's schedule as they walked to the car. "A place called Zuma Beach."

Since she'd never been to Los Angeles before, she didn't know much about the beaches, but Trevor did. According to him, Zuma Beach was one of the most popular and biggest beaches in that part of California. Because it was so close to Hollywood, it was also a popular film location. In fact, several of the beach scenes in his television series LA Beat had even been filmed there. Since she was such a fan of the show, Addison made a mental note to see if she recognized the beach. Who was she kidding? She wasn't going to recognize any silly old beach. She'd been so focused on Trevor, LA Beat could have been filmed on Mars and she wouldn't have known it.

Trevor was right about the beach being popular. Though from the number of bikini-clad girls clustered around the cordoned-off area where the magazine was doing the photo shoot, Addison suspected they were there more to see Trevor than to play in the surf.

While Trevor went off with the reporter from Men's Fitness to do the interview, Addison hung back to make sure Leo knew where to pick her and Trevor up after the photo shoot, then did a quick communication check with the hand-held radio he'd given her. When she was done, Bob showed her how to program the radio to monitor mode.

"It lets me listen in to whatever is going on at your end," he explained. "If you and Trevor ever get into a sticky situation and need me, just switch the radio to monitor to let me know you're in trouble and I'll come running."

Her brow furrowed. "Has that ever happened before?"

"Just once. Sophia had to turn the radio to monitor and drop it in her purse while she tried to help Trevor get away from a mob of college girls. Apparently, it was some sorority dare where they had to steal his underwear. They got pretty violent about it, too."

Addison's eyes went wide. "Oh God, that sounds horrible. Was everyone okay?"

Bob nodded. "Yeah, but it was touch and go there for a while. Luckily, Trevor doesn't wear underwear. As soon as they figured that out, they decided to high-tail it out of there."

Addison felt her face color at the thought of Trevor going commando underneath those snug-fitting jeans he wore. Mumbling something about checking on Trevor, she told Bob and Leo she'd see them later, then hurried over to the cabana where the reporter was doing the interview.

They were just finishing up when she got there. Trevor gave her a smile as he got to his feet.

"I'm going to check in with wardrobe," he told her. "You can wait over by where the photographer and the rest of the crew are set up if you want to watch the photo shoot."

Addison almost laughed. Of course she wanted to watch the photo shoot! As she watched Trevor make his way toward wardrobe, she couldn't help but wonder what kind of clothes he was going to change into for the pictures.

Eager to make sure she had a good view, Addison slipped off her shoes and walked across the sand to where the photographer and the rest of the photo crew were waiting. She was all ready to say she was Trevor's personal assistant when they asked who she was, but since no one questioned her presence, she assumed they must have seen her come in with Trevor.

Addison had never been to a photo shoot before, but since she had every magazine Trevor had ever been featured in, the opportunity to actually go behind the scenes was even more exciting. She just hoped they didn't have him posing with some bikini-clad model. That would just spoil the whole thing.

She glanced around, looking for one, when she spotted two girls standing over by one of the lights. While attractive, neither of them were wearing bikinis, which meant they clearly weren't models. They were talking about Trevor, though. Curious, Addison took a step closer so she could hear better.

"You got to do Matthew McConaughey last time," one of the girls said. "That means I get to do Trevor Braden."

Addison's eyes narrowed. Despite the fact she was Trevor's assistant and had no claim on him, she couldn't help the little stab of jealousy that went through her at the thought of him having sex with either girl. They weren't even his type!

"Or," the other girl said with a smile, "we could both oil him down."

The first girl giggled. "Oooh, a Trevor Braden sandwich! I like it!"

Addison almost laughed. The girls weren't talking about sleeping with Trevor; they were talking about rubbing him down with oil for the photo shoot! Addison frowned. Not that she liked the idea of the two girls running their hands all over him any more than she liked the idea of them jumping into bed with him. A Trevor Braden sandwich? Not if she could help it!

Shoes dangling from her hand, she walked over to the two girls and gave them a smile. "Sorry to interrupt. I'm Addison, Trevor Braden's personal assistant." She gestured to the plastic bottle one of them was holding. "Is that by any chance the bottle of oil I'm supposed to use on Trevor for the photo shoot?"

The girl's brow furrowed in obvious confusion. "Well, yes, but we're supposed to put it on for him."

"I know, but Trevor asked me if I'd do it." Addison shrugged apologetically. "I am his personal assistant, after all and it's kind of in the job description. I could get fired if I don't do it."

The girls exchanged looks and for a moment, Addison thought they might make a scene, but to her relief, they surrendered the bottle of oil without protest. Giving them another smile and a "thank you," Addison turned to see Trevor making his way across the beach.

Though Addison had seen him wear swim trunks in the movies before, it wasn't the same as seeing him in the flesh, and her pulse sped up wildly at the sight. It had to be illegal for a guy to be that gorgeous.

Addison was so caught up in all those sculpted muscles of his that she completely forgot she was supposed to rub oil on him until the photographer practically shouted for it. From the perturbed look on the man's face as he said the words, she had the feeling it wasn't the first time he'd tried to get her attention. Her face coloring, Addison hurried over to where Trevor stood.

He must have expected a make-up girl to do the rub-down because he lifted his brow.

The ocean breeze had pulled a few strands of hair free from the bun at the nape of her neck to blow them across her face and she reached up to nervously tuck them behind her ear as she gave him a smile. "The make-up girls were fighting over which one of them would get to rub you down, so in the interest of keeping the peace, I thought it might be better to do it myself. If that's okay with you, I mean?"

Trevor regarded her in silence for a moment as if wondering whether to believe her story or not, but then the corner of his mouth edged up. "It's okay with me if it's okay with you. It's not really in your job description, though, so I understand if you don't want to do it."

Want to? It was fantasy come true!

Addison tried to be as professional about rubbing Trevor down with the oil as she could, especially since they had an audience, but it was impossible not to get all hot and bothered. As she ran her hands over his broad shoulders and muscular chest, then down his six-pack abs, it was all she could do not to tear off her own clothes and rub the oil on with her naked body. Between her legs, her pussy purred at the thought.

Stifling a moan, she kneeled down so she could do his legs and found herself eye level with his crotch. For the second time that day, she completely forgot about the bottle of oil in her hand. All she could do was stare at his package and think how she was in the perfect position to give him a blow-job. A little tug on those navy blue swim trunks and...

"I can get the rest, if you want."

Addison jerked her head up at the words to see Trevor gazing down at her and she blushed.

"Wh-what? Oh, that's okay. I'm good." She was better than good; she was in heaven. She smiled up at him. "I'm almost finished." That was true. Another minute or two and she'd be having an orgasm.

Squeezing more oil into her hand, she ran her hands up and down his well-muscled legs, then repeated the process again, a little more slowly this time. As she did so, she tried not to look at his crotch, but she couldn't help sneaking a peek from the corner of her eye all the same. Though she wasn't sure, it looked like he had a more significant bulge going on in those sexy swim trunks than he had before. Could it be that he was as turned on by her touching him as she was? Her pussy tingled at the thought.

Addison would gladly have spent the rest of the day rubbing Trevor down with oil, but he was already glistening in the mid-afternoon sun. Picking up the bottle, she reluctantly got to her feet. Resisting the urge to run her hands over those muscular pecs one more time, she gave Trevor a smile, then turned and walked over to stand with the rest of the crew.

As she watched Trevor switch from one manly pose to the next for the camera, Addison made a mental note to find out which issue of Men's Fitness the photos were going to appear in so she could pick up a copy. She thought she caught him looking at her several times while he was posing for the camera, but then told herself she was probably imagining it. She was standing in back of the photographer, after all. Even so, it still made her knees weak.

An hour into the photo shoot, the photographer told everyone to "take five" so the crew set up on a different part of the beach. While they did that, Trevor went back to wardrobe to change into a different pair of swim trunks. That gave Addison the opportunity to rub him down with oil again, something she did quite eagerly. She promised herself she wasn't going to wash her hands for a week!

The second half of the photo shoot was more of the same, this time with Trevor doing sporty action stuff with a football and a Frisbee at the water's edge. Watching the way his muscles flexed as he tossed the football around excited her so much it was all she could do not to slip her hand underneath her dress and touch herself.

It was late in the day by the time they were done, and though she'd spent most of it sitting under a canopy, Addison was still exhausted. In contrast, Trevor didn't seem tired at all, which made no sense since he had done all the work. Then again, rubbing a hot guy down with oil, then watching him make eyes at the camera all day was a very strenuous job. Her lips curved into a smile at the silly thought. If that was work, she'd be willing to do it for the rest of her life.

When they got back to the mansion, it was to find that Maribel had already gone home. She'd left dinner in the oven for them, however, much to Addison's delight. After spending the day at the beach, she was starving. Whatever the other woman had made, it smelled delicious.

"Want to stay for dinner?" Trevor asked Bob as he opened the cabinet to grab some plates.

Bob shook his head. "Nah, I got a date with this new girl I met. Thanks anyway." He gave Addison a smile. "You two have fun."

As she listened to the bodyguard's cheerful whistle fade down the hallway, Addison had the sneaking suspicion Bob didn't have a date at all. He hadn't stayed because he wanted her and Trevor to have dinner together. Maybe Bob thought it would improve their working relationship.

Work, however, was the furthest thing from Addison's mind. That probably had something to do with the fact that Trevor suggested they have dinner at the kitchen table instead of the breakfast bar, then insisted she sit while he serve the casserole Maribel had made. As she sat across from him in the cozy breakfast nook a few minutes later, she could almost believe they were on a date.

"Was that your first time at a photo shoot?" Trevor asked as he sipped his wine.

She nodded. "I never realized that standing in front of the camera could be such hard work."

He chuckled. "You get used to it."

62

"Well, you're a natural at it." She picked up her glass of wine and took a sip. "Did you always want to be an actor?"

His mouth quirked. "I wanted to be a football player. But my mom made a deal with me when I was in high school. If I wanted to go out for football in the fall, then I had to try out for the school play in the spring. Believe me, if I hadn't wanted to play wide receiver in the NFL so bad, I would have said forget it. But I figured what the hell? So, I kept my end of the bargain and tried out for the play. I'd planned to flub my lines miserably, so my mom would get off my back, but once I got there, I actually started to get into the whole acting thing. Of course, it helped that I read for the part opposite this really cute girl."

She laughed. "Of course. So after that, you were hooked, huh?"

He nodded. "Completely."

As they ate, Addison listened with fascination as he described how he'd come to Hollywood and how difficult it was getting into the movie business. While Maribel had told her how Trevor had gotten his big break on the television show LA Beat, she loved hearing the story again from him.

"So, what about you?" he asked when he'd finished.

"Me?"

He leaned forward, his mouth twitching. "Yeah. Did you always want to be a personal assistant?"

If he only knew! "Oh, that. No. I went to college for liberal arts and just kind of stumbled on the whole personal assistant thing."

He flashed her a grin. "Lucky for me."

Maybe it was the sexy look in Trevor's eyes or maybe it was the silky way he said the words, but whatever it was, it made Addison catch her breath. For one wild moment, she thought he might lean across the table and kiss her. Good heavens, what was she thinking? Trevor was her boss! Actors did not get involved with their personal assistants.

Abruptly realizing he was looking at her expectantly, Addison cleared her throat and sat back in her seat. "It's getting late. I should probably go up to bed."

Trevor glanced down at his watch, lifting a brow when he saw what time it was. "Yeah, me too."

She pushed back her chair. "I'll help you clean up."

He shook his head. "That's okay. You go up to bed. I can take care of this."

"Are you sure? I don't mind."

He smiled. "I'm sure. Have a good night."

"You, too."

Addison got to her feet, then pushed in her chair. Giving him a smile, she murmured something about seeing him in the morning before heading for the door. As she made her way up the stairs, she found herself wishing she had stayed and talked to Trevor some more. But between the wine and the intimate setting, she'd let herself forget who she was. If she wanted this job to work out, she needed to keep things professional with Trevor. But knowing he was sleeping just down the hall from her made that extremely difficult. She groaned. Oh heck, now how was she supposed to get any sleep with thoughts like that running through her head?

With a sigh, she pushed open the door of her bedroom and went inside. Hoping a shower would take her mind off her handsome boss, she stripped off her clothes and headed for the bathroom.

But as she ran her soapy hands over her naked body a few minutes later, she couldn't help thinking about rubbing Trevor down with oil on the beach that afternoon. Her pussy quivered at the thought and she let out a little moan. Rather than push the images from her mind, though, she leaned back against the tiled wall of the shower and let them play out.

In her fantasy, she and Trevor were alone on the beach, and he was the one applying the oil. She closed her eyes as she pictured him rubbing his strong, slick hands up and down her naked body. Beneath the spray, her nipples hardened and she cupped her breasts in her hands, imagining they were Trevor's.

Between her legs, her pussy began to throb and she ran one hand down to finger her clit, pretending it was Trevor who was touching her. She caught her lower lip between her teeth as she imagined him bending his head to kiss her.

She pictured him sliding his oily hand over her hip to cup her ass as he thrust a finger deep inside her. She began to move her own fingers faster and faster on her clit, pretending they were his.

Oh yeah, Trevor, she thought. You're going to make me come.

But just as she felt herself start to climax, the Trevor in her fantasy lifted his hand and smacked her on the ass!

Her eyes flew open and her orgasm faded as she jerked her fingers away. Okay, where the heck had that thought come from?

Pushing the stray image of Trevor spanking her from her mind, she closed her eyes and plunged back into her erotic fantasy before her orgasm completely disappeared altogether.

This time she was bent over with Trevor sliding his big, hard cock into her from behind. She moaned and rubbed her clit faster. But the moment she got close to coming, Trevor spanked her on the ass again!

Annoyed, Addison almost stopped rubbing her clit a second time, but she was just too damn close to coming. She closed her eyes and pressed her fingers hard against her clit, making small circles round and round the plump, little flesh. As she played with herself, she tried to make her fantasy go where she wanted, but no matter what she did, Trevor continued to spank her.

Deciding it was easier to simply give in to the fantasy, she let herself go with it. She imagined Trevor pumping into her, his hand coming down over and over again on her ass as she cried out with pleasure.

The orgasm that coursed through her body was so intense she was actually dizzy from it and she had to grab the shower head to steady herself as her climax continued to wash over her. She'd never come so hard in her life.

By the time her orgasm subsided, all she could do was lean back against the wall while the water from the shower cascaded down on her. How could she come so hard from a little fantasy, especially one that involved Trevor spanking her?

Not sure she wanted to know the answer to that, Addison turned off the water and stepped out onto the bath mat. As she grabbed one of the fluffy towels and wrapped it around her, she couldn't help glancing in the mirror to check to see if her bottom was red. Of course it wasn't. But the spanking had felt so realistic in her fantasy, she wasn't sure.

Quickly drying off, she went into the bedroom and slipped into bed. Despite how tired she was, however, she didn't fall asleep right away. All she could do was think about the fantasy she'd had in the shower. While she couldn't deny it had been hot, she wasn't sure what it said about her? Why would any modern, independent girl like to get spanked by a guy? She's was still trying to figure that out as she drifted off to sleep.

Chapter Four

The next week flew by. Between getting Trevor to photo shoots, interviews, auditions and meetings, Addison didn't have time to think about the crazy fantasy she'd had about him spanking her. Which was probably a good thing, considering every time she looked at her boss an image popped into her head of her draped over his knee with him warming her bottom. It was distracting, to say the least. She didn't know how she even managed to get her job done.

Somehow, though, she did get it done. And she was getting better at it every day. Amazingly, she had finally figured out how to juggle Trevor's endless list of commitments. That probably had something to with the fact that she'd learned how to multi-task. It also helped that she programmed the calendar on the computer to send her reminders not just days before an event, but hours and minutes before, too. It might seem extreme, but it worked. And although she never would have believed it after her first day on the job, she actually loved what she was doing. She could definitely see herself making it a career.

It wasn't only the work or her newfound ability to do the job that made being a personal assistant fun, though. It was her adopted family, or at least that's how she was coming to think of them. There was Maribel, the concerned mother; Bob the supportive, sometimes teasing brother; Leo, the trustworthy uncle; even Murray played a role as the demanding father figure.

Since she lived right there in the mansion, Addison ended up spending almost all of her free time with them. Well, everyone except Murray, that is. The rest of them would sit around the table in the kitchen with her, talking and laughing about anything and everything. She couldn't remember having as much fun with her own family. They had never been that close.

It was even more fun when Trevor joined them around the table, which he did more often than not, much to Addison's delight. Of course, she didn't consider him a brother, like she did Bob. She definitely liked to think of their relationship as something a little bit more intimate.

Although Addison was determined to keep her relationship with Trevor professional, that was getting harder and harder to do. Not only did they spend eighteen hours a day together, but he usually spent most of that half-dressed. If he wasn't hanging by the pool in a pair of swim trunks, then he was walking around the house all hot and sweaty after a workout. It was enough to make any girl lust after him.

On average, she decided she fantasized about having sex with Trevor at least once an hour. And when she did, most of her fantasies involved him spanking her at some point. She tried to tell herself it was wrong for a modern, independent woman like she was to want a guy to spank her. But after four days of vivid fantasies accompanied by at least that many amazing orgasms courtesy of her trusty vibrator, she gave up trying to fight it. As a result, she couldn't walk into the kitchen without imagining Trevor reddening her ass with one of Maribel's big wooden mixing spoons or sit in a seat without picturing him bending her over it for a sound spanking.

Biting her lip to stifle a moan, Addison determinedly thrust her erotic daydreams to the back of her mind and forced herself to focus on the calendar on her computer. She quickly scanned the schedule and saw that although Trevor was free the rest of the afternoon, he was hosting a society charity event to benefit several of LA's homeless shelters that evening. A week ago, she would have been hyperventilating at the thought of pulling off something that big, but now she was more than confident she could handle it.

She smiled as she remembered how passionate Trevor had been when he'd told her about the benefit. She was actually a little surprised to hear how involved he was in his charity of choice, but he knew from experience how many kids with stars in their eyes came to Hollywood to be a movie star like him and instead ended up living in one of those shelters. The look in his eyes and passion in his voice made only made her fall for him that much harder.

Wanting to make sure everything was perfect for the event, Addison went into the kitchen to talk to Maribel. While outside caterers would be providing the hors d'oeurves as well as the open bar, the older woman would be overseeing everything to make sure it ran smoothly.

"I've got it all covered, dear," Maribel assured her with a smile. "Just relax."

Addison promised she would. Right after she checked in with Bob about security and parking. When she finally tracked him down, he told her the same thing Maribel had.

"I'm all over it." He gave her a wink. "Relax."

Regardless of how much confidence she had in Maribel and Bob, Addison would rather have stayed downstairs and supervised the preparations anyway. But as Trevor's personal assistant, she needed to be at the party, not working it. Which meant she had to change into something more glamorous than the tailored slacks and blouse she was currently wearing.

Looking at the clothes in her closet a few minutes later, however, she wished she'd thought to add "go shopping for a new dress" to her list of things to do for the party. But since she hadn't, one of the dresses she'd brought with her would have to do. Picking out a simple, but sophisticated looking wrap dress, she set it down on the bed, then went into the bathroom to shower and freshen her make-up.

An hour later, she was regarding her reflection in the full-length mirror. While she was sure the black dress wasn't nearly as elegant as the ones the actresses at the party would be wearing, it still showed off her slender curves and long legs nicely. She might be the hired-help, but that didn't mean she couldn't look hot all the same.

Giving herself one more look in the mirror, Addison left her bedroom to head downstairs. She was just walking past Trevor's room when the door opened and he stepped out. She stopped in mid-step, all coherent thought suddenly impossible at the sight of him in a tuxedo.

She'd seen him in a tux on the red carpet at the Oscars and other award shows, of course, but that had been on television. In person, he looked good enough to eat.

Abruptly aware of how underdressed she must look next to him, Addison felt her face color. She really should have gone shopping.

"You look beautiful," Trevor said.

She knew he was probably just saying that to be nice, but it made her feel good anyway. "Thank you. You look pretty good yourself."

Pretty good? He looked hot as hell! But she supposed she couldn't very well say that to him. He was her boss, after all.

Trevor grinned. "Thanks. Shall we go downstairs?"

* * *

As they descended the steps, it occurred to Addison that this was the first Hollywood party she was attending and her pulse quickened. Meeting all the celebrities she'd only seen on television or in the movies would be exciting. She was definitely looking forward to it.

70

But just as everyone began to arrive, Murray appeared out of nowhere and pulled her off to the side before Trevor could even introduce her to anyone.

"What the hell do you think you're doing?" he demanded.

She frowned, taken aback by the sharp tone in his voice. "My job."

His mouth tightened. "Your job is to be available if Trevor needs you, not to steal the limelight from him. He's the star, not you. Now go do something that is your job, like check on the caterers."

Addison's face flamed at the rebuke. Before she could say something in reply, however, Murray strode off to position himself at Trevor's side. Her lips curled. Apparently, that little rule about not stealing the limelight from Trevor didn't apply to Murray himself.

Afraid the manager might make a scene if she didn't do as he told her, Addison tried to make herself as inconspicuous as possible for the rest of he evening. She stood in the corner of the room, sipping champagne and watching Trevor move from person to person, shaking hands and telling jokes. She'd never seen anyone work a room like he did.

Two hours into the party, Trevor made a speech about the charity he was supporting and announcing he would match each and every donation with a contribution of his own. That surprised Addison. She already knew Trevor was generous by the way he treated the people who worked for him, but to match everyone's contributions dollar for dollar was truly altruistic. And expensive. Murray looked like he was going to have a cow after the announcement.

As Trevor mingled with the guests again, Addison realized Murray was no longer at his side. She looked around the room for the manager, but didn't see him anywhere. She'd wanted to compliment Trevor on his generosity the moment he finished his speech, but didn't want to risk another confrontation with Murray. Since the weasel wasn't in sight at the moment, however, it was the perfect opportunity to talk to Trevor. And if Murray came over to interrupt them, she'd simply say she was checking to see if Trevor needed anything.

Taking a glass of champagne from a passing waiter's tray, Addison started to make her way over to Trevor when she saw a tall, dark-haired woman sidle up to him. Addison immediately stopped in her tracks as she recognized Cindi Adams. Heiress to a multi-million dollar company, she was one of those people in Hollywood who had a reality show on cable and thought that made her an actress. She was simply famous for being famous. And for her huge breasts, of course, as well as her willingness to show them off to anyone and everyone. She was known for being at any affair where there were cameras, booze and hot guys. Apparently, the hot guy she was interested in tonight was Trevor.

Addison's hand tightened on the glass in her hand as she watched Cindi practically drape herself all over him. Her plastic boobs were in serious danger of falling out of the indecently low-cut white gown she was wearing. Maybe OSHA should slap a warning sticker on those things; they could hurt someone.

"She certainly likes to put on a show, doesn't she?"

Addison turned to see Maribel standing beside her. "Yes, she does. Can't she tell that Trevor isn't the least bit interested in her?"

Maribel shook her head. "I doubt she's the type who notices if a man is interested or not. Or even cares, for that matter."

Addison thought the older woman was probably right. "I have half a mind to walk right over there and dump this champagne right down the front of that trampy dress she's wearing."

Maribel laughed. "Well, if you're going to do that, don't waste your time with champagne. Get a glass of my cranberry rum punch. It'll leave a better stain."

Although it was extremely tempting, Addison resisted the urge. "I can't. It would only make a scene and Trevor doesn't need that tonight."

"You're probably right. Though you putting that hussy in her place is something I would pay to see." The other woman sighed. "I'd better get back in the kitchen. Enjoy the rest of the party."

Addison wasn't sure how she could enjoy the party with the way Cindi Adams was pressing her entire body up against Trevor. Addison wondered why he didn't put some space between him and that inflatable love doll. As down-to-earth as he was, she couldn't believe he would actually be interested in someone who was so obviously fake. Then again, he was a man and not many men could refuse a not-so-subtle overture like the one Cindi Adams was making.

Ignoring the queasy feeling in her stomach that watching the two of them gave her, Addison lifted her glass to take a sip of champagne only to pause with it halfway to her lips as Cindi Adams deliberately put herself in the way of an actor who was walking by just so she could fall against Trevor when the other man bumped into her. Trevor had no choice but to throw his arms around her or they both would have ended up on the floor. Cindi giggled girlishly and clung to him as if she was stranded in the middle of the ocean and Trevor was a life preserver.

"Oh, hell no," Addison muttered. The bimbo wasn't getting away with that. Two could play her little game.

Setting her champagne down on a nearby waiter's tray, Addison grabbed the glass of cranberry rum punch before heading across the room. As she made her way over to where Trevor was standing with Cindi, she was tempted to just walk up to them and throw the drink right in the

73

other woman's face, but decided against it. That would be way too obvious. So instead she waited until she almost reached them, then pretended to trip, propelling herself - and the drink – forward. The cranberry red liquid not only drenched the front of Cindi Adams' expensive white gown, but also splashed onto the considerable amount of cleavage she was showing as well.

The look on Cindi's face as she stared down at the red stain on her designer gown was priceless and Addison had to put her hand to her mouth to hide her smile.

"Oh God! I'm so sorry! Let me get something to wipe that up." She grabbed a stack of cocktail napkins off the table closest to them and held them out to the woman. "Here, take these. I'll go get some club soda from the bar."

Cindi stared at her in disbelief. "Napkins and club soda aren't going to get rid of this stain, you twit! My gown is completely ruined!" She fixed Addison with a nasty glare. "You did that on purpose, didn't you?"

The words seemed to echo in the huge room and everyone had stopped what they were doing to stare at them. Addison saw Trevor's eyes narrow and she quickly feigned a look of surprise. "Of course not. I tripped on the carpet."

"Tripped my ass!" Cindi Adams snarled.

Addison opened her mouth to protest, but the words turned into a startled gasp as the other woman let out a shriek and threw herself at her. Addison instinctively took a step back, but Trevor stepped between her and the enraged heiress, catching her with a hand on either arm.

"Okay, that's enough. Let's not make a scene," he said firmly. "My assistant didn't mean to spill her drink on you. She tripped."

Cindi struggled against his hold, her eyes flashing with anger. "Like hell she didn't! Let go of me so I can show that bitch what happens when someone messes with me!"

Even though Addison knew there was no way the other woman could get past Trevor, she took another involuntary step back anyway. This was going to get ugly. She was just wondering if she should get security when Bob showed up with two rent-a cops that had been hired for the event.

Although he kept a firm grip on her, Trevor ignored Cindi Adams' tirade as he glanced at Bob. "Do me a favor and see that Cindi's driver takes her home, would you?"

"My pleasure."

At Bob's nod, the two men with him immediately stepped in to take hold of Cindi Adams' arms, one on either side of her. That didn't cool her down, though. On the contrary, made even more of a spectacle of herself as they escorted her from the room, shouting threats at Addison all the way to the door.

Once the heiress and her two escorts were out of sight, Trevor turned to the other guests, all of whom were still standing in stunned silence.

"Okay, folks," he said. "That concludes this evening's entertainment. You can go back to enjoying the rest of the party now."

To Addison's surprise, the awkward silence that hung over the room disappeared to be replaced by the soft murmur of conversation. It was if the whole bizarre confrontation between her and Cindi Adams had never happened.

Travis turned to her, his eyes full of concern. "Are you okay?"

Addison gazed up at him, both touched and a little surprised by the worry she saw on his face. She half expected him to take her arm and march her upstairs to give her a spanking for purposely spilling her drink on that bimbo. The thought sent a shiver of excitement running through her.

"Addison?" he prompted when she didn't say anything.

She felt her face color. "I'm fine. Just a little freaked, I guess. She looked like she wanted to scratch my eyes out."

His mouth tightened. "Don't worry about it. By tomorrow, she'll be thrilled that it happened. Remember, for someone like her, any publicity is good publicity."

Addison wasn't so sure about that. Cindi Adams had seemed really pissed to her.

Trevor regarded her in silence, then let out a sigh. "Look, why don't you take a break for a little while? Go into the kitchen to see if Maribel needs any help with the caterers."

Addison opened her mouth to tell him she didn't need a break, but closed it again when she spotted Murray making his way over to them, his face absolutely apoplectic. On second thought, she could use a break, after all.

She gave Trevor a smile. "Maybe that's a good idea. If you need anything, just yell."

Turning, she hurried down the hall and into the kitchen, where she found a smiling Maribel waiting for her.

"You saw?" she asked the older woman.

"No, but I heard about it." Maribel laughed. "I wish I'd seen the look on that bimbo's face."

Addison's lips curved. "It was pretty priceless. Right up until the moment she tried to scratch my eyes out."

"Trevor came to her rescue, though."

Addison turned at the sound of Bob's voice to see him coming up behind her. "You were there?"

"I headed for the living room as soon as I heard the sound of raised voices." He grinned. "If you wanted that skank to stop hanging all over Trevor, all you had to do was say the word. I would have tasered her."

76

She blushed. While she wouldn't have minded that, she didn't want Bob to think she was jealous of the woman. "I don't know what you're talking about. I tripped."

He laughed. "That's your story and you're sticking to it, right? Wow, maybe you ought to go into acting."

Maribel made a tsking sound. "Pay no attention to him, Addison. Bob, don't you have security to see to or something?"

When he didn't move, she made a shooing motion with her hands. "Go on. Off with you now."

"Okay, okay. I know when I'm not wanted." Giving Addison a wink, he turned and left the kitchen.

Addison gave Maribel a sidelong glance, waiting for the woman to comment or worse, elaborate, on what Bob had said. But instead, the cook merely muttered something about Bob being a terrible tease and went off to talk to one of the caterers. With a sigh, Addison leaned back against the counter and picked up an hors d'ouerves from the tray beside her. Regardless of what Maribel said about Bob and his penchant for teasing, she had the feeling the bodyguard knew way too much for his own good. She hoped he didn't say anything to Trevor about it. That would be beyond embarrassing.

Addison hung out in the kitchen until she was sure everyone at the party had forgotten about her confrontation with Cindi Adams before going back into the living room. The rest of the evening wasn't nearly as eventful and though Murray glared at her from across the room, he didn't come over to talk to her, much to Addison's relief.

By the time the last of the guests left, it was well after two. Stifling a yawn, Addison checked with Maribel to see if she needed any help in the kitchen. When the older woman said she didn't, she went back into the living room to find Trevor talking to Bob in the entryway. Hoping Bob wasn't ratting her out, she gave the men a wave and told them to have a good night before hurrying upstairs to her room.

Too tired to bother taking a shower, Addison hung up her dress in the closet and tossed her underwear in the hamper in the bathroom. She was just getting ready to brush her teeth when there was a knock on the door. Brow furrowing, she put down her toothbrush and grabbed her short robe from the hook on the wall. She slipped it on as she walked into the bedroom, then tied the sash around her waist before opening the door.

She blinked in surprise. "Trevor!"

"Can I come in?"

She stepped back, opening the door wider. "Of course."

Addison shut the door after he came in, then turned to give him an apologetic look. "Sorry I disappeared after the party. I should have checked to see if you needed anything before I came upstairs."

He shook his head. "That's okay. I didn't need anything. I just wanted to talk to you about what happened earlier before I went to bed."

Her brow furrowed. "You mean about what happened with Cindi Adams?"

He nodded. "You spilled your drink on her on purpose, didn't you?"

Addison stared at him in stunned silence, unable to believe he'd caught on to her charade. Dammit. Well, she wasn't going to admit anything.

"Of course not," she said. "Why would I do something like that."

He shrugged. "You tell me."

She blushed. Tell him she was jealous of that slut? Not a chance. She lifted her chin. "Look, if you're going to spank me, let's just get it over with."

Addison didn't know which of them was more surprised by her words. She couldn't really say what had made her blurt out such a crazy thing. Maybe all the erotic fantasies she'd been having the past week. She stifled a groan. Well, it was out now. And if he wanted to spank her, she wasn't going to complain.

Trevor lifted a brow. "Spank you?"

She gave him a shrug. "That is why you came to my room, isn't it?"

The corner of his mouth edged up. "Actually, no it isn't. But now that you mention it, I probably should spank you."

Her pulse skipped a beat. "For tripping and spilling my drink on some bimbo?"

"Bimbo, huh?" His mouth twitched again. "I guess that means I was right. You did do it on purpose."

Addison opened her mouth to deny it, but Trevor had already taken her hand and was leading her over to the bench at the foot of the bed. Excitement surged through her. Although she knew she should protest like she had the other times, she couldn't make anything come out. Right then, she didn't trust herself to speak.

So, she said nothing as Trevor sat down and guided her over his knee. As he put his hand on the small of her back, it abruptly occurred to her just how short her robe was. In this position, it rode up the backs of her thighs until it was barely covering her ass. While her face colored at the thought of Trevor seeing her bare bottom, she couldn't deny the sexy little thrill it gave her at the same time.

Even though she wanted this spanking, she couldn't help but tense as she waited for the first smack. When it came, she let out a gasp as his hand connected sharply with her right cheek. Then before she could catch her breath, he delivered another smack to the opposite cheek. He went back and forth from one side to the other, his hand falling with a steady rhythm that had her ass burning almost immediately.

And yet despite how much the spanks stung, she was getting excited as hell. She had been half afraid that when Trevor put her over his knee, she would focus so much on the sting of the spanks that she wouldn't get as aroused as she had in her fantasies. But if anything, the sting that went along with the spanking seemed to get her even more turned on than her fantasies had, and she had to bite her lip several times to keep from letting out a moan.

As she began to squirm more and more slowly in an effort to grind against Trevor's leg, Addison wondered if he could tell she was getting excited. From the way his hand lingered on her ass after each smack, she thought for sure he must. That thought got her even hotter and she found herself wishing he would flip up her short robe and spank her on the bare bottom. That would be unbelievably erotic.

But to her dismay, after one more well-aimed spank to each cheek, Trevor took her arm and gently set her back on her feet. As he got to his own, she reached back with both hands to cup her freshly spanked ass. Her pussy throbbed so much it was all she could do not to slid her hand between her legs and touch herself right there in front of him. The idea of him watching her get herself off was so hot that she had to stifle another moan.

She resisted the urge and forced herself to stand there obediently as he lectured her about her behavior at the party. Though she tried to pay attention to what he was saying, she couldn't seem to focus. All she could do was stare at that sensuous mouth of his and wonder what it would feel like on her own. She wondered what he would do if she put her arms around his neck and kissed him. Would he kiss her back? And if he did, would they end up in bed? She was tempted to give into the urge so she could find out.

"Is that understood, Addison?"

She blinked at the question. Giving herself a mental shake, she forced herself to give Trevor a nod. "Yes, completely. I won't do it again."

Trevor regarded her in silence, his expression unreadable. Then the corner of his mouth quirked. "Good. Because if you do, the next time I'm going to lift up that short robe of yours and spank you on the bare bottom."

Addison blushed. Oh God, had he read her mind? Of course not. That would be impossible. But since he had made the threat, she was already trying to figure out what she could do to get herself spanked again just to se if he would go through with it.

Chapter Five

Fifteen minutes later, Trevor stood in the ice cold shower, willing his hard-on to go away. But it was no use. The big guy had a mind of his own and right now that mind was preoccupied with thoughts of Addison's rosy red bottom. Damn, he'd never been this aroused in his life. He had already been standing underneath the cold spray for at least ten minutes and his shaft hadn't softened one bit. He was beginning to think that as long as Addison was his personal assistant, this just might be a permanent condition.

He hadn't really gone into Addison's room with the intention of spanking her. He still couldn't believe she'd brought it up. But once she had, he hadn't been able to resist putting her over his knee. When she hadn't protested, at first he'd thought it was simply because she had resigned herself to a spanking. But then she had started squirming around on his lap. Not in discomfort, but in pleasure. Then she'd let out those breathy, little moans and it had almost been his undoing. God, they had to be the sexiest sounds he'd ever heard.

It had taken every ounce of self-discipline not to pull up her short robe and see if she was wearing any panties underneath. But he'd restrained himself. Just barely. And in reward for his willpower, she had wiggled on his lap again, which made her robe ride up even higher, and he'd been treated to a glimpse of her perfect ass cheeks. He still hadn't been able to tell if she'd been wearing any panties, though.

He'd still caught his breath at the sight. In fact, he was so entranced that he almost forgot he was supposed to be spanking her. When he finally got his wits about him again, he had found himself caressing her ass in between smacks. Then he'd followed that up by fantasizing about sliding his hand between her beautiful legs and touching her pussy. Just thinking about her sighs of pleasure had almost been enough to make him come.

He had gotten control of himself at the last moment, though. Pulling her off his lap had been the hardest thing he had ever done in his life, but somehow, he had managed it. He had even remembered to scold her for her behavior and warn her not to do it again.

He still didn't know how he'd resisted the urge to sweep her up in his arm and take her to bed. The only thing that had stopped him was knowing how completely wrong sleeping with her would be. Addison worked for him and he didn't want to put her in a position where she felt she had to have sex with him to keep her job. He had met too many scumbags in Hollywood who did just that and he'd promised himself he would never be like them. So, he had fought the urge to take her to bed and instead come back to his room to take a cold shower.

He put both hands against the imported tile wall and dropped his head, letting the water course down his back. Who the hell was this woman who had him so out of control?

As he stood there trying to answer the question, it suddenly came to him that despite her vehement denial, Addison had almost certainly spilled her drink on Cindi Adams on purpose. He just didn't know why. There were only two reasons he could think of. One was that Cindi had said something to Addison earlier to make her mad enough to throw her drink at the actress. He didn't see how that could be, though, because Cindi had been hanging all over him from the moment she'd gotten to the party and therefore couldn't have spoken to his personal assistant. Which left the other reason. Addison had spilled her drink on the actress just so he would put her over his knee and spank her.

But that was crazy, wasn't it? Then again, considering the moans of pleasure she'd been making while he'd been spanking her, maybe it wasn't so crazy after all.

Holy crap!

Why the hell hadn't he seen it before? Because he'd been too busy getting turned on by all the wiggling and sexy sounds she was making for a thought as logical as that to register.

As he stood there underneath the cold spray of the shower, another even more startling realization came to him. Maybe the reason Addison liked his spankings so much was because she liked him.

If he was right about that, what would have happened if he had given in to temptation and kissed her? Would they be in her bed right now? An image popped into his head of a naked Addison lying beneath him, her legs twined tightly around his body as he pumped into her.

Trevor let out a groan and reached down to wrap his hand around his rock-hard cock. He closed his eyes and moved his hand up and down, imagining it was Addison touching him. He pictured her there in the shower with him, her naked body glistening with water as she stroked his shaft. Man, what an image!

Then he pictured her kissing her way down his chest and abs until she was kneeling between his legs. In his fantasy, Addison looked up at him with big, blue eyes, then leaned forward to take his cock in her mouth. The vision of her on her knees giving him a blow job was so damn hot that he couldn't hold back any longer. As much as he would have liked to spend the rest of the night right there in the shower fantasizing about his beautiful personal assistant, he found himself tightening his grip on his cock and moving his hand up and down faster and faster. A moment later, his orgasm exploded through him. He threw back his head and let out a hoarse groan, shuddering with pleasure as cum splashed onto his hand.

84

When he was done, he leaned back under the cold water and let it run down his body again. Fantasizing about Addison while he'd jerked off had been damn fun, though not nearly as much as he imagined the real thing would be.

But would sleeping with her be any more acceptable even if she was attracted to him? She still worked for him. If the feelings were mutual, though, surely that would be enough for him to bend the rules, wouldn't it?

Trevor swore under his breath. What was he talking about? He didn't even know for sure if Addison was attracted to him or not.

So, find out, a little voice in his head whispered.

But how?

Right then, he wasn't sure. But he hoped it would have something to do with spanking her beautiful bottom again.

Just thinking about having her over his knee had him sporting an erection again. With another groan, Trevor threw himself directly under the shower's spray and turned the cold water up to full blast.

* * *

The next morning, Addison quickly showered and dressed, then went downstairs to grab some breakfast before getting to work. Despite getting to bed so late the night before, she felt surprisingly refreshed. Maybe because Trevor had given her a spanking. The memory made her shiver with pleasure and she had to bite her lip to stifle a moan as she walked into the kitchen. She glanced at her watch, wondering if she had enough time to run up to her room an give herself a quick orgasm. Probably not. Damn.

Marisol wasn't in the kitchen, but Murray was and he looked fit to be tied.

"There you are." He intercepted her halfway to the coffee pot and held the entertainment section of that morning's newspaper up in front of her. "Look at this! What the hell did you think you were doing?"

Addison looked at the paper. There was a full-color picture of Cindi Adams running out of Trevor's house with a big, red stain on her low-cut dress.

Murray lowered the newspaper. "You're not mentioned by name because you're not worth mentioning, but Trevor sure as hell is. It implies he had a member of his staff throw a drink on Cindi Adams to force her to leave the party. Her people are furious. And so am I. This could cost Trevor big and it's your fault."

Addison lifted her chin. "I didn't mean to do it, you know. It was an accident."

"Oh, sure it was!" Murray's brows drew together. "What were you thinking? Did you figure if Cindi Adams left, Trevor would look at you? Forget it, girl. He's out of your league. I don't even know why he keeps you around. You're incompetent as a personal assistant. If it was up to me, I'd fire your ass in a second."

Addison opened her mouth to tell him to go to hell when a voice interrupted her.

"Good thing it's not up to you then. And since Addison works for Trevor, just like you do, it's never going to up to you."

Addison turned to see Bob coming into the kitchen. He was dressed in jeans and an Oregon State T-shirt. He gave her a grin and walked over to stand beside her.

"Bye, Murray," he said.

The other man opened his mouth, but only sputtered something under his breath, then turned on his heel and left.

"Don't worry about him," Bob said. "He's an A-hole."

Addison laughed. "You're right. He is. I appreciate you getting rid of him for me. He can be kind of intimidating."

86

Bob opened a cabinet and took out two coffee mugs. "Don't worry about him. Trevor is the guy you need to impress and I think you've already done that."

Addison grimaced. "I'm not so sure about that. Not after last night and that disastrous episode with Cindi Adams."

"Don't sweat it. None of us thinks much of her anyway, including Trevor, so the fact that you got rid of her makes you tops on everyone's list around here."

"Even Trevor's?"

Bob glanced at her as he poured coffee into the mugs. "Even his. Of course, he won't admit it because he has this horrible tendency to think only the best of everyone. Which is why he probably has no idea you intentionally spilled your drink on that plastic bimbo."

She lifted a brow. "You really think so?"

Bob handed her one of the mugs. "I know so."

Addison let out a sigh. "That's a relief. I wouldn't want to give him any reason to fire me."

"Trust me, that's not going to happen." Bob took out the container of creamer from the fridge and set it on the counter, then did the same with the sugar bowl. "You may not realize it, but Trevor is really taken with you."

"Really?" She frowned. "I wouldn't have thought that." Especially not after all the spankings he'd given her, she added silently.

Bob stirred sugar into his coffee. "That's because you don't know him as well as I do yet. Take it from me. He likes you."

Addison considered that as she slid onto one of the stools at the granite island. "You two seem like really good friends. How long have you known each other?"

"Since grade school. We rode the same bus, had the same classes, and got into a lot of the same trouble." Bob grinned and leaned back against the counter beside the fridge. "Then in high school, we played on the same football team. I was the blocking tight end and he was the star wide receiver. We both made it to Oregon State on scholarships. Trevor could have been a star, but he paid a lot more attention to school than I did. He actually learned something in college whereas I just played ball. But I tell you, when he was in the game, I mean really in the game, nobody could slow him down. He helped get the Beavers to the Fiesta Bowl our senior year. We completely trounced Notre Dame."

Addison laughed. She remembered reading a magazine interview where Trevor had mentioned something about playing football in college.

"I love football. My college team wasn't good enough to go to any bowl games, but we won a few. And the mascot was so cute. He was this goofy looking hound dog and every time the team scored a touchdown, he ran up and down the sidelines in front of the stands waving this huge dog bone while the band played Who Let The Dogs Out. It was hilarious."

Bob didn't laugh, but instead studied her over the rim of his mug with an amused look. "If you're going to fib about who you are, you're going to have to start being a little more careful with the details than that."

Her heart stopped. "Wh-what do you mean?"

"You said your college mascot was a hound dog. The mascot for Brown University is a bear."

"Brown...?"

"Yeah. Brown University. Like it says on your resume. You know, the ivy league school you supposedly went to?"

Addison felt her face go red and quickly lifted her mug to take a sip of coffee. "Brown. You're right, it is a bear. I can't believe I forgot. I must have been thinking about the games I went to at one of the neighboring colleges."

Dammit, how could she have been so stupid? If Trevor found out she wasn't who she claimed to be, she could kiss her job as his personal assistant good-bye. She only hoped Bob didn't call her on it. But no such luck.

"You don't have to keep lying," the bodyguard said. "I've known for a long time that you aren't an ivy league brat."

Her hand tightened around the mug. The coffee she'd just drunk churned in her stomach. She felt like she was going to be sick. "H-how did you know?"

"Well, for one thing, you don't act like a stuck-up snob." He grinned. "And for another, you work too hard to be an ivy leaguer. Not that they don't know how to work hard, it's just that they usually don't have to. Plus, I'm in charge of security. It's my job to know these things."

She swallowed hard. She was busted. "Does Trevor know?"

"Know what? That you aren't an ivy leaguer or that you're pretending to be your sister?"

Addison's heart sank. She'd hoped Bob had just thought she had lied about what college she'd gone to, but it was worse than that. He knew she had lied about who she really was. Tears stung her eyes and she blinked them back.

"How did you figure it out?"

"I run a background check on everyone who works for Trevor. Brown University had a graduate by the name of Madison Mattingly, but no Addison." The bodyguard shrugged. "I did some more digging and learned that she's your sister. I figured you used her name because you thought she had the better resume."

He was half right, at least. Madison did have the better resume. Addison wondered if she should try to explain that Madison was the one who had taken the job only to bail on Trevor at the last minute, but then decided against it. What would be the point? She had lied and in the end, her reasons for doing it didn't matter.

"You're going to tell Trevor, aren't you?" she asked in a small voice.

"Hell, no. Why would I?"

Her eyes went wide. "Why wouldn't you?"

"Because you're doing a great job. And because he's happier than he's been in a long time. Like I said, he's taken with you." Bob gave her a wink. "Besides you're fun to have around. But that doesn't mean you shouldn't tell Trevor yourself."

Addison stared at him incredulously. He couldn't be serious. How could she tell Trevor she'd been lying to him all along?

"Bob's right, you know."

Addison swiveled around on her stool to see Maribel coming into the kitchen.

"You know, too?" Addison asked.

"Of course I do. I'm very observant." On the other side of the kitchen, the bodyguard lifted a brow. Maribel made a face. "And Bob told me. But that doesn't change the fact that you need to tell Trevor before it's too late."

Addison frowned. "Too late for what?"

Maribel took a carton of eggs out of the fridge and set them down on the counter. "Before you two start to develop real feelings for each other."

Addison stared at the older woman in astonishment. What was the woman talking about? Maribel made it sound like she and Trevor were having a relationship.

"Maribel's right," Bob said. "You and Trevor need to develop a relationship based on honesty if you want it to work."

She blinked. Had they both lost their minds? And when had Bob the bodyguard become Bob the love doctor? "Relationship...?"

"Yes, a relationship. And not of the working variety, either." Maribel gave Addison a smile as she took a mixing bowl out of the cabinet. "Don't think we haven't noticed the way you look at Trevor. And if you weren't so silly, you would have noticed that he looks at you the same way."

Her pulse skipped a beat. "He does?"

Maribel opened her mouth to answer, but closed it again as Trevor abruptly came walking into the kitchen. Addison blushed and quickly looked down at her coffee mug. How much of their conversation had he heard?

"Why'd everyone get so quiet?" Trevor asked. "You talking about me again?"

"How'd you guess?" Bob quipped. "I was just telling Addison about our college football days. Turns out, she's a huge fan of the game."

Trevor looked at her in surprise. "Seriously?"

Addison nodded and murmured something in agreement, though she could quite say what it was. All she could focus on was what Maribel and Bob had said. Could Trevor really be just as smitten with her as she was with him? The idea that a hot, hunky movie star like him might be attracted to a plain, little nobody like her was ludicrous. He had his pick of every actress, supermodel and heiress within a thousand miles. Maribel and Bob had to be wrong.

But even though she told herself they were imagining things, Addison couldn't stop from daydreaming just a little about what it would be like if it were true and Trevor really was interested in her. The thought alone was enough to make her heart beat faster.

In fact, she was so immersed in her fantasy world that she almost forgot Trevor had to be at the studio that afternoon to shoot one final pick-up scene for his big, new action movie. The premiere was set for that weekend, so the director was already cutting it close by refilming the scene and she didn't want to stress everyone out even more by getting Trevor to the studio late.

For his part, Trevor didn't seem stressed out at all, though, not even when traffic made them a few minutes late. Relieved he wasn't mad, Addison went to find a place to stand along the fake LA street so she could watch the filming along with the rest of the crew.

While she waited for Trevor to come out of his trailer, Addison listened with half an ear as the group of men beside her talked about what a nice change of pace it was to be extras in an action movie instead of some boring old commercial. She couldn't help but smile as she glanced at them. Dressed in business suits and carrying briefcases, they looked like they'd just come from a meeting. One of the men, a tall dark-haired man with gray at his temples, looked familiar, but she couldn't place where she'd seen him. Since he went on and on about how many television commercials he'd been in, she decided it was probably in one of those.

By the time Trevor came out to film his scene ten minutes later, she gave up trying to figure out where she'd seen the other man and concentrated on her boss instead. She always had fun watching Trevor work and today was no exception. In the scene, Trevor's character was meeting with his contact on a busy downtown street. They had originally filmed it on location in LA, but according to Trevor, the director wasn't happy with how the LA background noises had completely stomped on all of the dialogue, so they were redoing it. Even though she and Trevor had gotten to the studio a few minutes late, everything else went off without a hitch. The director didn't even have to tell her to be quiet during filming like he'd done the other day, although he did give her a warning look a few times.

After they wrapped up, Addison chatted with the crew while she waited for Trevor to change clothes. Everyone right down to the assistant to the assistant of the production assistant was excited about the premiere. Addison had to admit she was pretty excited herself. Of course, she wouldn't get to walk the red carpet or anything, but she'd be able to wait in the background, watching the monitors with the other assistants and production crew. That was good enough for her.

Trevor was unusually quiet on the drive back to his mansion. Addison wondered about it, but then decided he was probably just tired from filming. She was starting to get a little tired, too, which wasn't surprising considering she'd gotten to bed so late the night before. Thinking about the spanking her gorgeous employer had given her after the party guests had left made her pussy spasm and she squirmed on the seat. Any more thoughts like that and she was going to have to run to her bedroom for some quality time with her vibrator the moment they got back to the house.

However, when they got home, Trevor asked if he could speak to her in private. Addison couldn't very well refuse, no matter how much her pussy was demanding attention, and would have led him to her office, but he had already started up the stairs. She followed as he led the way to his bedroom, wondering if he needed help picking out another shirt or something. Even though that was almost certainly what he wanted, she felt a little flutter in her tummy as he closed the door behind them.

She dragged her gaze away from the huge king-size bed to look at him.

"We were late getting to the studio today," he said as he walked over stand in front of her.

He said the words casually, but for some reason, the tone in his voice did funny things to her pulse.

She reached up to tuck her hair behind her ear. "Yeah, I know. I'm sorry about that. We would have been on time if there hadn't been so much traffic."

"LA's famous for its traffic. If we'd left earlier, we would have been on time. But because we didn't leave earlier, the crew was forced to wait for us."

Addison wondered if she should point out that they were only five minutes late and that neither the director nor anyone else on the crew had been annoyed. But Trevor spoke again before she could decide.

"I can't let this slide, you know that, right?"

It suddenly dawned on Addison why Trevor had brought her to his room. He was going to spank her again! Why the heck had it taken her so long to figure that out? Because Trevor was acting completely different than he had the other times he'd spanked her. He wasn't the least bit upset she'd messed up. In fact, he looked almost pleased she'd given him a reason to put her over his knee again. As if he enjoyed spanking her as much as she enjoyed getting spanked. A slow fire spread over her whole body at the possibility. The warmth settled in the space between her legs and her pussy quivered.

Abruptly realizing he was waiting for an answer, she blushed and nodded. "I know. And you're right. I should have thought about the traffic and had us leave earlier. It was my fault we were late. I suppose I should...probably be spanked."

She felt her face flush even more as she said the words. She couldn't believe how easily they'd rolled off her tongue. It was like someone had given her a script. Which wasn't too far off, she supposed. Being here in Trevor's bedroom was like something out of a movie. Or her wildest fantasies.

"I think you're right," Trevor said.

He took her hand and led her over to the upholstered bench at the foot of the bed. Sitting down, he guided her over his knee so that she was stretched out across his lap. Her pulse quickened as he placed a firm hand on the small of her back. The simple action was enough to send a quiver of excitement through her, and she had to bite her lip to stifle a moan.

Addison held her breath as she waited for Trevor to begin, but instead he surprised her by gently rubbing her bottom through her skirt. She let out a soft sigh of pleasure, unable to help herself. Something told her this spanking wasn't going to be like the others he'd given her.

Abruptly, Trevor lifted his hand and brought it down on her right cheek with a loud smack. Despite having experienced a spanking before, Addison still gasped.

"Was that too hard?" Trevor asked.

She lifted her head to look over her shoulder at him, surprised by the question. The other times he'd spanked her, he hadn't asked if the smacks were too hard. But then again, this wasn't like the other times.

"No," she said. "You just caught me off guard. You can keep spanking me."

The corner of his mouth lifted. Blushing, she quickly turned back around. No sooner had she done so than she felt him deliver a sharp smack to the other cheek. He moved back and forth from one cheek to the other like that until her ass felt warm and tingly all over.

That wasn't the only part of her anatomy that was tingling, either. Her pussy was positively purring.

She got even more aroused when she felt Trevor slowly push up her skirt. She caught her breath as his fingers brushed the edges of her skimpy bikini panties. She wondered if he would pull them down, but instead he caressed her ass cheeks through the silky material. She'd thought the massage he had given her over her skirt had been fun, but feeling his hand on her almost bare bottom was exquisite. She could only imagine how much more amazing his touch would feel when he pulled down her panties. If he pulled them down, of course. She shivered with anticipation at the thought.

Lifting his hand, Trevor brought it down hard on her right cheek. Without her skirt for protection, the spank stung a lot more than the ones before, and she couldn't stifle the little yelp that escaped her lips. Trevor's hand came down again, this time a little harder and she squirmed on his lap.

"Owwww!" she squealed.

This time, Trevor didn't stop to ask if he was spanking her too hard, but simply continued to deliver firm smacks to each cheek with a slow, steady rhythm that made her ass feel as hot as if she'd sat on a stove. God, the man knew how to spank a girl. Not to mention get her aroused. If he ever did touch her, she'd probably combust! The thought made her moan.

Then all at once Trevor stopped spanking her. For a minute, Addison thought he might be done, and she opened her mouth to tell him not to stop, but then she felt him hook his fingers in the waistband of her panties and slowly slide them down until they were banded around her thighs. As he did, she realized they were wet with her arousal.

She waited breathlessly for Trevor to caress her ass cheeks like he'd done after he pushed up her skirt, but instead he lifted his hand and brought it down on her bare bottom with a resounding smack. Addison hadn't realized how much protection her tiny panties had given her until now, and as he spanked her over and over, she squealed and squirmed.

Despite her protests, however, Addison didn't want Trevor to stop. The more he spanked her the more turned on she got and before long, she was wiggling as much in an effort to grind her clit against his jean-clad thigh as she was from the stinging smacks.

It felt so amazing Addison thought she might actually be able to make herself come like that. But just then, Trevor stopped spanking her to give her ass a firm squeeze. The feel of his hand on her freshly-spanked bottom made her gasp out loud.

"Your ass is so red," he said softly. "And your skin is so hot."

As he spoke, his fingers lightly brushed the underside of her derriere and she moaned. It occurred to her then just how close his fingers were to her pussy and before she even realized what she was doing, she spread her legs as much as the panties around her thighs would allow.

"Touch me," she begged. "Please."

The words were out before she could stop them, but it was too late to take them back. She wouldn't have even if she could. Right then, she didn't care that he was her boss or how inappropriate her request was. She had dreamed about making love with Trevor from the first time she'd seen him on television and she wasn't about to pass up the chance to fulfill it. Besides, if he didn't touch her, she thought she might just go insane.

Fortunately, she never had to find that out because Trevor slid his hand between her legs and ran his finger teasingly along the slick folds of her pussy.

"Is this how you want me to touch you?" he asked.

She let out another moan as his finger glided along her lips. "Yes."

"You're very wet, do you know that?"

She murmured something unintelligible, unable to manage more than that.

He dipped his finger in her pussy before running the tip up and down her slit again. "I think you must have liked that spanking. Am I right?"

"Mmmm," she breathed.

"I didn't hear that. Did you say you liked it?"

"Oh God, yes. I loved it!"

He must have approved of her answer this time because he found her clit in the downy curls and made little circles on it with his fingers. Addison made a soft sound of appreciation that was somewhere between a sigh and a moan.

"Would you like me to make you come like this?" Trevor asked.

Addison ground against his hand. "Yes!"

She wasn't sure whether she was rotating her hips in time with his fingers or whether it was the other way around, but he brought her to orgasm faster than she ever would have thought possible and she cried out as ripples of pleasure coursed through her. Afterward, all she could do was lay there draped over his knee and try to catch her breath while Trevor coaxed the last little bit of tremors from her body. When he had, he took her hand and gently helped her to her feet.

Addison reached up with one hand to brush her long hair back from her face. Standing there in front of him with her ass still stinging from a spanking, her panties banded around her thighs and her body still trembling from the amazing orgasm he'd just given her, she decided she'd never felt sexier. Then again, perhaps that had something to do with the smoldering look Trevor was giving her.

"You have no idea how much I want to take you to bed right now," he said hoarsely.

Her lips curved into a smile. "So, what's stopping you?"

He opened his mouth as if to answer, but then closed it again. With a groan, he got to his feet and swung her up in his arms in one smooth motion, then walked around the bed to set her down on the middle of it. She gasped as her tender ass cheeks came into contact with the sheets, but the sound was lost as he bent his head to cover her mouth with his. Trevor's kiss was everything she'd dreamed it would be, only better. It was passionate, breathtaking and intoxicating, and she murmured her approval against his mouth as she wrapped her arms around his neck and kissed him back. When he finally lifted his head, all she could do was gaze up at him.

Trevor reached out a hand to smooth her hair back from her face. "I've wanted to do that since the first time I saw you standing on my doorstep."

She blinked. "You have?"

He nodded, the corner of his mouth edging up into a devastating smile. "Yes."

"Then why didn't you?"

"Because I didn't want to take advantage of you."

Addison wanted to tell him that he wasn't taking advantage of her, but as he captured her lips in another searing kiss, she decided that what she'd been going to say could wait. All she could think about was the incredible things his tongue was doing to hers.

Trevor's hands moved to her sleeveless blouse, undoing the buttons and pushing it off her shoulders before reaching around to unclasp her bra. Her breasts spilled eagerly into his hands, her nipples hard with excitement, and she sighed with pleasure as he made lazy, little circles around them with his thumbs.

"Does that feel good?" he asked.

"Mmmm-hmm," she murmured.

Addison arched against him, hoping he would bend his head and take one of her nipples in his mouth. To her delight, Trevor took the hint and as his lips closed over the sensitive peak, she could only moan. He suckled, tugged and nibbled until she thought she would go crazy from how good it felt, and when he finally lifted his head, it was to do the same to the other nipple and drive her wild all over again. He definitely knew his way around the female anatomy, that was for sure.

Giving her nipple one more flick of his tongue, Trevor lifted his head to gaze down at her. The desire she saw in his eyes made her catch her breath and she could only lie there as he slowly pulled her skirt over her hips and down her long legs. Her panties quickly followed and a moment later, she was completely naked before him.

"God, you're beautiful," he breathed.

Trevor Braden, the hottest actor in Hollywood, thought she was beautiful? An almost ridiculous sense of pleasure surged through Addison at the compliment. She wanted to thank him, but the ability to speak disappeared as he unbuttoned his shirt and all she could do was stare as his muscular chest and six-pack abs came into view. She'd never seen a guy more gorgeous in her life. The memory of how incredible those muscles had felt under her hands when she'd rubbed oil on him for that photo shoot the other day made her want to reach out and touch him, but he was already unbuttoning his jeans and pushing them down his well-muscled legs. As his thick, hard cock sprang free, her pussy spasmed. She caught her lower lip between her teeth. Mmmm, he was going to feel so good inside her.

Without taking his eyes off her, he opened the drawer on the bedside table and took out a foil-wrapped packet. She licked her lips with anticipation as he took out the condom and rolled it onto his hard shaft. Giving her a sexy grin, he climbed on the bed and braced a hand on either side of her head as he settled himself between her legs.

As the tip of his cock touched the opening of her pussy, Addison ran her hands up his smooth chest to grasp his shoulders. Her breathing quickened as she waited for him to enter her. But to her dismay, he didn't slide inside right away, Instead, he slowly rubbed the head up and down her wet slit. Her pussy throbbed with need and she let out a frustrated moan.

"Stop teasing me," she said huskily. "I need you inside me. Now!"

When Trevor didn't obey right away, she thought she might actually have to resort to begging, but just as she was about to open her mouth, he slid inside her in one smooth motion that made her gasp.

"Dear God, you feel good," he rasped.

Her lips curved into a smile. "So do you."

Wanting him inside her as deep as he could go, she wrapped her legs around him and pulled him closer. She'd

100

never had a man fill her so completely before. It was breathtaking.

Trevor didn't thrust immediately, but stayed nestled deep inside her and she tightened her hold on his shoulders, tugging him down for a kiss. She sighed in appreciation as his tongue slow danced with hers. She'd been right to envy his on-screen leading ladies. He was a great kisser.

As he explored her mouth, Trevor slowly began to thrust his cock in and out. Addison instinctively lifted her hips to meet his, matching his rhythm. Each time her still tender ass came down on the bed, it reminded her of the spanking he'd given her, and she undulated her hips faster and faster.

Addison's breath came in quick pants the closer she got to coming, and she had to drag her mouth away from Trevor's. His breathing was just as ragged and he bent his head to bury his face in the curve of her neck, pumping into her harder.

"Don't stop," she begged him breathlessly. "Please don't stop!"

"I won't, baby," he promised. "I'm going to make you come, just like this."

Her orgasm began to build even as he spoke the words, and Addison threw back her head and screamed over and over as wave after glorious wave of ecstasy washed over her. As the sound echoed around the huge room, she only hoped it didn't carry to the rest of the house. But then Trevor let out a deep groan as he found his own release and she decided she didn't care if everyone in Hollywood heard. This was the most special moment of her life and she wasn't going to regret any of it.

When their breathing had returned to something resembling normal, Trevor rolled onto his back, taking her with him.

"That was amazing," she said softly.

He pressed a kiss to the top of her head. "You're the one who's amazing."

The words made her feel ridiculously happy and she wanted nothing more than to lay there in the warmth of his arms and bask in their glow, but she knew she couldn't. What they had shared had been incredible, but she was still his personal assistant. She needed to get back to her own room before another member of the staff found them together.

She lifted her head from his chest and gave him a small smile. "I guess I should be going to my room."

Trevor gently twirled the end of her long hair around his finger. "Or you could just stay here."

Her pulse skipped a beat. She hadn't expected that. "You mean sleep with you?"

His mouth twitched. "Among other things. If that's okay with you."

Was he kidding? This night was getting better and better. She smiled. "It's very okay with me."

He grinned. "Good."

Wrapping his arm around her, he pulled her down for another one of those scorching kisses. Addison let out a sigh as she kissed him back. This was like a dream come true. She only hoped it wasn't really a dream and she woke up the next morning to find herself in her own bed.

Chapter Six

Addison wasn't sure what woke her the next morning, but she closed her eyes again and snuggled into her pillow so she could go back to sleep. Only it wasn't a pillow she was lying on. It was something much firmer and definitely more solid. Trevor's chest. Last night hadn't been a dream.

She and Trevor had made love. And it had been even better than in her fantasies.

No way. She must be dreaming. She had to be dreaming.

Her eyes flew open again, only this time she jerked upright to see if she really was in bed with Trevor or whether it was just wishful thinking, and found herself gazing down at her gorgeous employer.

She really hadn't been dreaming.

Addison took in his chiseled jaw and wide, sensual mouth. Asleep like this with his hair all tousled and his arm carelessly thrown over his head, he looked younger and even more handsome, if that was possible.

Images of all the erotic things they'd done the night before flashed into her head and she had to bite her lip to stifle a moan as her pussy spasmed. They hadn't made love just once, but several times, and each time had been even more amazing than the one before. Her wildest fantasies hadn't prepared her for how truly hot Trevor was in bed.

But while Trevor might have wanted her in his bed last night, that didn't mean he wanted one of the staff walking in to find them together this morning. Resisting the urge to lean over and give him a kiss, she started to slip out of bed when she felt a gentle hand on her arm.

Addison turned to see Trevor regarding her with sleepy eyes. Damn, he looked scrumptious first thing in the morning.

"Where are you running off to?" he asked.

She reached up to push her hair back from her face. "I just thought I should go before someone came in and found me here."

He frowned at that, but didn't say anything. Then he gave her hand a tug, gently pulling her into his arms. "People don't just walk into my bedroom unannounced, so you don't have to worry about running off. At least not until I get to give you a good morning kiss."

Before Addison could reply, Trevor slid his hand in her hair and covered her mouth with his. She melted against him, all thoughts of anyone walking in on them vanishing as his tongue slow danced with hers.

He ran his free hand over the curve of her breast, cupping its softness in his palm and giving the nipple a firm squeeze between his thumb and forefinger. She murmured her approval against his mouth. Mmm, she loved when a guy paid attention to her nipples.

Still kissing her, Trevor urged her onto her back. She went willingly, sighing as he trailed light kisses along her jaw and down her neck to her breasts. Cupping them in his hands, he closed his mouth over one nipple, suckling on it gently before slowly swirling his tongue round and around the peak. Even though Addison was sure that she would go mad from such exquisite torture, she still let out a moan of protest when he finally lifted his head. Until she realized the only reason he had stopped lavishing such glorious attention on that nipple was so that he could do the same to the other.

Flicking her nipple with his tongue one more time, he released her breasts to continue his exploration of her body, slowly kissing his way down her stomach to her belly button. Once there, he stopped to make teasing, little circles

104

around the indentation with his tongue before dipping it inside. Addison caught her breath at the sensation. She'd never had a man pay so much attention to that part of her body before, and she had no idea it could be so erotic.

As much fun as that was, however, Addison forgot all about what he was doing to her belly button when he moved lower. Her breathing quickened as he got closer and closer to the juncture of her thighs.

Cupping her ass in his hands, he ran his tongue up the slick folds of her pussy once, then twice, before finally closing his warm mouth right over her clit. He flicked the sensitive nub with quick, light flicks of the tongue, then made lazy, little circles round and round it.

She moaned and threaded her fingers in his thick hair. "Oh God, just like that," she breathed. "Don't stop!"

He didn't. Instead, he tightened his grip on her ass cheeks and continued to do that delicious, little circle-thing with his tongue again, only more firmly this time. The sensation was so intense that she wanted to scream, but her cries were trapped in her throat as her orgasm began to build. It started right at her clit, then gradually spread through her entire body until she was trembling all over. She writhed beneath him, moving her head from side to side on the pillow with a moan as he wrung every bit of pleasure from her.

As her orgasm subsided, all Addison could do was lie there and try to catch her breath as he pressed a gentle kiss to the inside of her thigh. She had never been with a guy who was so talented with his tongue, or one who could make her come so fast.

Kissing his way back up her body, Trevor settled himself between her legs. His hard cock poised at the opening of her pussy, he braced himself on his hands and gazed down at her for a long moment before capturing her mouth in a searing kiss. As his tongue tangled with hers, he rubbed the head of his cock up and down her slit over and over.

"Stop teasing me, Trevor," she begged him. "Please!"

He obeyed, slowly easing himself into her wetness in one smooth motion. Addison gasped against his mouth as he filled her pussy, wrapping her arms and legs around him to pull him in even deeper.

Trevor made love to her slowly, sliding his penis all the way out of her pussy, then back in again. With each thrust, she got closer and closer to another climax. She was sure Trevor was on the verge of coming, too, but when she tried to urge him to thrust faster by lifting her hips, he only continued his slow, easy rhythm.

Then, without warning, he rolled onto his back, taking her with him. Addison blinked, surprised by the move, but excited by it, too. She'd never had a guy do that before.

Trevor let her sit there for a moment, allowing her to catch her breath before he slowly began to thrust into her pussy.

"Ride me," he commanded softly.

Placing her hands on his chest, Addison slowly moved up and down on him, lifting all the way up before sinking back down on his hard length again. The motion drove his cock deeper and deeper inside with every thrust, and she moaned.

She was just getting into a rhythm when she felt Trevor's hand smack her ass. Startled, she let out a little yelp of surprise. But as a delicious warmth spread over her bottom, her lips curved into a sexy, little smile.

"Mmm," she breathed. "Do that again."

Beneath her, Trevor's eyes danced as he lifted his hand to spank her ass again. Even though she knew it was coming, Addison let out another little squeal as the smack landed squarely on her already stinging ass cheek.

106

"Keep riding me," he ordered, his hand coming down on her other cheek.

Addison squealed again, but did as he ordered, moving up and down on his hard cock in time to the rhythm of his spanks. Each time he smacked her ass, her pussy clenched tightly around his shaft, sending little shivers of pleasure through her body.

Trevor continued to spank her, alternating from one cheek to the other, delivering smack after stinging smack until he finally grabbed her burning ass cheeks with both hands and began pumping into her wildly.

She gasped at the feel of his strong hands squeezing her tender bottom. "Harder!" she cried. "Fuck me harder!"

He obeyed, gripping her ass and pumping into her so forcefully that she couldn't have stopped herself from orgasming even if she had wanted to. She came with such soul-shattering intensity that she thought she might actually faint from how incredible it felt. Beneath her, Trevor groaned long and low as he found his own release, Knowing he was coming with her only made her own orgasm that much stronger and she cried out even louder.

Afterward, all she could do was collapse forward to lie on his chest and try to catch her breath. They stayed like that, his arms around her, neither one of them saying anything. Addison would have been content to spend the whole day there, but then a loud, embarrassing growl from her stomach interrupted the moment.

Trevor chuckled, the sound a deep rumble beneath her ear. "I guess someone's hungry."

She laughed, her face coloring. "Maybe a little."

He tilted up her chin to give her a kiss. "Come on. Let's go see what Maribel made for breakfast."

By the time she and Trevor showered, however, it was well past breakfast and already lunchtime by the time they got downstairs. Of course, that probably had something to do with the fact that Trevor pulled her into his arms for a long, drugging kiss the moment they stepped under the spray of the shower. They'd ended up having sex again, this time with her bent over and him taking her from behind. She could definitely get used to waking up like that every morning.

The fact that she and Trevor had both "overslept" wasn't lost on Bob and Maribel. As they ate, the bodyguard and cook peppered her and Trevor with teasing, little comments like, "I guess you two must have sleep well last night," and "You would think with that much sleep, you two would look more refreshed, but you look exhausted."

She and Trevor acted as if they had no idea what the man and woman were talking about, but it was hard not to smile from here to Texas. Addison had enjoyed last night's extra-curricular activities immensely and definitely hoped for more of the same in the evenings to come.

But then it struck her that Trevor hadn't confessed their budding relationship to Bob and Maribel. What if he hadn't mentioned it because he was embarrassed? What if he had no intention of ever letting it go past anything more than sex? What if he only slept with her because she wasn't a Hollywood beauty? She'd read in Cosmo that some movie stars preferred to date women less attractive and famous than they were so they could feel wanted, powerful and sexy. What if Trevor was like that? The piece of tomato she was chewing suddenly got stuck in her throat and she swallowed hard.

Stop it, she told herself. She was being foolish. Trevor wasn't the type of guy to have issues like that. He was way too confident and secure. She was just doubting herself, like she always did. Sure, there was no guarantee that what they had would go anywhere, but then no relationship came with a guarantee. Maybe the reason Trevor hadn't said anything to Bob and Maribel was because he thought he had a shot of making something with her since she was genuine and real instead of some

108

Hollywood fake. She cringed inwardly at that. Okay, well maybe not so genuine. She was lying through her teeth to Trevor about who she was, after all. But she'd been honest about everything else, like how she felt about him. That was what mattered.

Beside her, Trevor flashed her a sexy grin, and Addison felt herself relax. Halfway through lunch, Leo came in to join them, and the conversation shifted from how late she and Trevor had slept to the pick-up shots he'd done at the studio yesterday.

Then she completely lost track of the conversation as she remembered the tall, dark-haired man who had been playing one of the extras. Yesterday, she had been sure she'd seen him somewhere, but hadn't been able to remember where. Suddenly, out of nowhere, the memory of where she had seen him before popped into her head. He'd been one of them men pictured on the front page of the website for Total Empire Investment Trust, the firm handling Trevor's investments.

She frowned. That didn't make any sense at all. Why would an investment firm hire an actor to play one of their executives? She must be mistaken.

Trevor reached under the table to put a gentle hand on her knee. "You okay?"

She blinked. "What?"

The corner of his mouth edged up. "You look like you were a hundred miles away. You okay?"

"Oh." She gave him a small smile. "I'm fine. I just remembered I have to confirm some interviews for you. I'll be right back."

His brow furrowed. "You don't have to do it right now. Let it wait."

"I can't." She gave him an apologetic smile. "I'll just be a minute."

Putting her napkin on the table, Addison pushed back her chair and hurried from the room before Trevor could stop her.

Once in her office, she closed the door and booted up her computer, then immediately logged on to the bank website, thankful that she still remembered the login and password. She scrolled down the page until she came to the investment links at the bottom. She took a deep breath and clicked on the one for Total Empire Investment Trust. A moment later, she was staring at the company's board of directors.

Holy crap, she'd been right. Right there, in the middle of the group, identified as Mr. Rutherford P. Chester III, Chief Financial Officer, was none other than the tall, dark-haired actor she'd seen at the studio yesterday.

Addison sat back. So, she was right, but what the hell did it mean? She really doubted the CFO of an investment company worked part time as an actor. It just didn't seem likely he was really a rich investment banker scratching an acting itch.

Which meant he was either Rutherford P. Chester's less-than-successful identical twin, or he really was an actor who had been hired by the investment company to play one of their executives. Being an identical twin herself, she knew she shouldn't discount the possibility, but instinct told her that wasn't what was going on here.

Maybe it was standard practice for companies to use actors to portray the real businessmen. Maybe the board members wanted their privacy. Either that, or they were too dishonest or sappy looking to get anyone to invest money. She chewed on her lower lip, considering the possibility, then shook her head. No, that just seemed too fishy.

Then a terrifying thought came to her. Oh God, what if the company was a front for something illegal, like money laundering? Stuff like that happened in movies all the time. Trevor could be involved in the whole thing and not even realize it.

Reaching for the phone, she dialed the company's number. Just to see if it was legitimate. A machine answered, stating that she had reached Total Empire Investment Trust, but that due to an incredibly high call volume, it was recommended she call back later or leave a message.

She hung up and stared at the computer screen. The more she thought about it, the more she was convinced that Total Empire Investment Trust was running some kind of scam. She needed to tell Trevor right away.

She was halfway to the door before she stopped. Maybe telling Trevor wasn't such a good idea. What if he thought she had been snooping into his financial affairs? Things were going so well right now and she didn't want to risk messing anything up by being a busybody. Maybe she should check into it a little more first before she said anything to him.

But how was she going to do that? She supposed she could Google the company or call the Better Business Bureau. Why do that, though, when she could simply go to the company's LA address and check things out herself?

Addison was just heading for the door when Trevor came in. He grinned.

"I was thinking we could spend the day together. Maybe take a drive or something. Just the two of us. What do you say?"

Addison caught her lower lip between her teeth. She couldn't believe she was going to turn him down, but finding out what was going on with this investment firm was too important.

"I'd love to, but I just remembered that I have to be somewhere."

He frowned. "Where?"

"Um, a meeting," she lied. "With the studio. About the premier."

"Call and tell them you'll meet with them tomorrow." He bent to nuzzle her neck. "Better yet, do it over the phone."

His lips brushed her ear and Addison had to bite her lip to stifle a moan. She was on the verge of saying the hell with playing private investigator and giving in to Trevor. But she couldn't. She was doing this for him. So, even though she felt horrible, she gently pulled away from him.

"I can't," she said. "I have to meet with them today. We can go for a drive when I get back if you still want to."

He sighed, but nodded. "Yeah. Sure."

She went up on tiptoe to kiss him. "I'll be back as quick as I can."

Ignoring the look of disappointment on his handsome face, Addison hurried out to the garage. Once there, though, she stopped. Dammit. She'd been in so much of a hurry that she hadn't even thought to check MapQuest for directions to the investment company. Unfortunately, she was terrible with maps and would never be able to find it without directions. Going back inside to look them up on the computer was out of the question, though. There was no way she'd have the strength to walk away from Trevor again, especially if he tried to talk her out of leaving.

She glanced over at Leo. He was washing the limo and hadn't seen her come in. As Trevor's driver, he probably knew all the streets in LA by memory. Hoping he'd knew where 2582 Condor Road was, she hurried over to ask him. Luckily, he knew where it was and gave her directions. Thanking him, she jumped in her car and left before he could ask any questions.

Even with Leo's directions, it took her a while to find the address. In fact, she drove by it several times, mainly because it was smack dab in the middle of the warehouse district and she was sure she couldn't be in the right area. But she was.

With a frown, she put the car in park and shut off the engine, then grabbed her purse from the seat beside her. Even though it was clearly an abandoned warehouse, she got out of her car and walked up to the front door anyway. She'd come all this way, after all.

"Can I help you, miss?"

Startled at the words, Addison jumped and spun around to see an older man dressed in a security uniform standing behind her.

She smiled. "I'm looking for 2582 Condor Lane. Is this it?"

He nodded. "Yes it is, but the place isn't occupied at the moment. If you tell what you're looking for, maybe I can help?"

Addison hesitated, unsure whether she should say anything. "I'm looking for Total Empire Investment Trust. Did they ever have offices here?"

His brow furrowed as he repeated the name. "I've worked here for fifteen years and I've never heard of the place. Are you sure you have the right address?"

She gave him another smile. "Seeing that it's an empty building, I guess not. I'm terrible with directions. Thank you."

Hurrying past him to her car, she pulled out of the parking lot and headed back the way she'd come, more curious and frustrated than before. Regardless of what she'd told the security guard, she was sure she had the right address, which meant the information listed on the Total Empire Investment Trust website was obviously bogus. She was willing to bet the phone number was fake, too. She could probably call from now until doomsday and never get a real person. But why would a company have a number that no one answered and give an address that led to nowhere? They wouldn't, not unless they were a front for something illegal.

Just then, a nagging thought struck her. What if Trevor knew all about it and was involved? She shook her head. No, she wasn't going to go there. Trevor couldn't be part of anything underhanded, he just couldn't. There had to be another explanation. Someone was clearly trying to pull something over on him. But who?

She nibbled on her lower lip as she sat in traffic. It was a long shot, but maybe the actor portraying the company's chief financial officer might know what was going on.

Taking a right at the next corner, she headed for the studio. There weren't a lot of people on the set since filming on the movie had wrapped, but luckily, she found a production assistant still hanging around. She was worried he might not know who she was talking about, especially since he had to think for a few minutes after she described the actor who had played one of the extras yesterday, but then he nodded.

"I think I have a name and address in the trailer," he said. "But I'm not sure I should be giving that out."

"I understand." She smiled. "It's just that Trevor really enjoyed working with him and thought he might like a part in Trevor's next movie. I'd hate for the guy to lose out just because I couldn't talk to him."

The production assistant was silent for a moment. "I could take your name and phone number and have him give you a call."

Damn. What now? "I really need to talk to him ASAP," she said. "You know Hollywood. The offer has a short shelf life."

The man sighed. "Tell me about it. Okay, hang on and I'll get you the info."

Unfortunately, Bill Worthington lived across town and it took forever to get there in LA traffic. It turned out

114

the actor lived in an apartment building that had seen better days. Even so, it was in the nicer part of the city.

Addison pulled into the parking lot and cut the engine, then got out of the car. Bill's apartment was on the second floor. Once she found it, she rang the doorbell and waited. To her relief, he opened the door immediately.

"Can I help you?"

Damn, Addison was hoping he'd recognize her as Trevor's assistant. She hurriedly introduced herself.

"I happened to see you on that investment company's website and thought you might know something about the place," she continued. "You know, whether it's a good company to invest with and stuff. I'm making pretty good money with Trevor and I figured I should be smart with it."

Bill frowned. "What investment company?"

"You know the one. Total Empire Trust Investment Group. Don't tell me you don't have the 411 on the place." She hesitated, then added, "Unless it's so good you want to keep it a secret."

"Total Empire...?" He clenched his jaw. "Son of a bitch! You actually saw the website? My damn agent said the company went out business before it even got up and running. I haven't gotten one damn penny for it." He swore under his breath. "I'm going kill that squirrelly agent of mine. I knew he was screwing me over."

Yikes! She hadn't realized he hadn't gotten paid for it. She needed to get him back on track, though. "So, you don't know much about the company, I guess?"

He shook his head. "I don't know anything about it. My agent didn't say much, just got me the job for the photo shoot. I wouldn't even have known who the photos were for if I hadn't overheard him talking to someone on his cell."

It was her turn to frown. "I don't understand. Wasn't there a name on the building?"

"We didn't take the photos in front of a building. We took them in front of a blue screen. My agent said the photos would be placed in different settings and see what worked best." He shook his head again. "I should have known something was up when I didn't recognize a single person on the set. All friends of my agent. Or that manager of Braden's, I suppose. In fact, I'm sure Murray was actually the one who set up the gig."

Her ear perked up at the name. "Murray?"

"Murray Sidle. My agent works with him occasionally. I've actually gotten a few gigs, thanks to him. Well, that's finished now. I'm calling my agent the minute you leave and telling that bastard I want my royalties. Do you have the link to the website? I'm going to need proof."

Addison's head was spinning. Murray was the one swindling Trevor? If he was, she couldn't let word get back to him that she was onto his scheme. She needed time to talk to Trevor.

It took some persuading, but fortunately, she was able to convince Bill to hold off on calling his agent.

"Okay," he said grudgingly. "I'll wait a few days. But then I'm going after my money. You might want to tell Trevor his manager is involved with a scumbag."

"Don't worry about that. I'm going to tell Trevor everything."

Thanking Bill, she left his apartment and headed back to Trevor's mansion. It was all starting to make sense now. Not only was Murray in the best position to create a fake company, but he had easy access to all of Trevor's money, too. Trevor would invest in anything Murray suggested. There was no telling how much of Trevor's money Murray had already stolen. But how in the world was she going to convince Trevor that his manager was ripping him off?

Chapter Seven

When she got back to the mansion, Addison didn't even bother pulling into the garage like she normally did, but instead parked her car in the circular driveway out front and ran inside. She skidded to a stop in the entryway when she saw Murray standing in the living room.

His eyes narrowed at the sight of her. "Where are you going in such a hurry?"

Her stomach clenched at his tone. Crap. He knew she'd figured out what he was up to. She didn't know how he knew, but she definitely knew. She could either tell him she'd learned he was a lying, thieving scumbag and have it out with him right then and there, or she could pretend she didn't know anything and let Trevor handle him. She decided to go with the latter. Murray worked for Trevor, after all.

She reached up to tuck her hair behind her ear. "Nowhere in particular. I was just heading to my office. I have to check Trevor's schedule and make sure everything is ready for the premier."

"Cut the crap!" he snarled. "I know exactly what you're up to, you little bitch. Didn't you think the security guard at the warehouse would call me?"

"Wh-what security guard?" she stammered. "I don't know what you're talking about."

"Like hell! As if that weren't enough, I get a call from that crappy small-time actor, Bill Worthington. He said you stopped by to see him. He told me you were over there asking all kinds of questions about Total Empire Investment and Trust."

Dammit! Bill Worthington had promised he wouldn't call Murray. She took a step back.

"Oh, that." She tensed to run, her hand tightening reflexively on the shoulder strap of her purse. "I heard he had some money with them and thought he might be able to tell me whether they were a good company to invest with."

His lip curled in a sneer. "You don't really expect me to believe that, do you?"

"I don't care what you believe. I don't know what you're talking about." She lifted her chin. "Now, if you'll excuse me, I have work to do."

Addison tried to go around him, but he grabbed her arm. "Not so fast. Who the hell do you work for? FBI? SEC?"

"I don't work for anyone but Trevor. And he's going to be mad as hell when he finds out you've been stealing from him, you toad." So much for playing it cool and letting her boss deal with Murray. "Now, let go of me!"

She jerked her arm from his grasp much easier than she would have thought. She didn't stop to question why he let her go, but instead turned and headed for the door. Or would have if she hadn't smacked into something solid and unmoving. She blinked as she realized it was a guy — a really big guy. And there was another one standing right beside him.

She instinctively took a step back, but with Murray behind her, she had nowhere to go.

"You may work for Trevor, but these men work for me," Murray said. "And they're not letting you go anywhere. Now, I'll ask one more time before I start to get unpleasant. Who do you work for?"

She whirled on him, intending to tell him to go to hell, but the sound of a car pulling into the garage stopped her. Trevor. Knowing she'd never make it to the door with Murray's goons standing there, she opened her mouth to scream for help instead. Murray's thugs must have anticipated the move because one of them grabbed her and slapped a hand over her mouth, muffling the sound.

"Take her to the warehouse," Murray ordered. "And make sure you use her car. I don't want Trevor finding it. I'll be there as soon as I can. Once I find out what she knows and who she talked to, we can get rid of her."

Addison's blood went cold at the words. Getting rid of her meant killing her, she was sure of it. Terrified as much by the prospect of what Murray intended to do to her as by the realization she would never see Trevor, much less anyone else again if Murray's thugs took her to that warehouse, she struggled like a mad woman to free herself. But it did no good. The man holding her wrapped his other arm around her waist and dragged her outside as if she were nothing more than a ragdoll.

* * *

To say Trevor was bummed that Addison had preferred to go to a meeting rather than spend the day with him was putting it mildly, especially since he'd given her permission as her boss to blow it off. He'd thought that after making love she would have been as eager to be with him as he was her. Clearly, he'd been wrong.

After she left, he went for a run on the treadmill to work off his frustrations, but it didn't do much good, so he went down to the local high school to throw the football around with Bob instead. They'd barely walked onto the field before his friend brought up Addison.

"I thought you and Addison would be spending the day together," Bob said, tossing the ball up in the air, then catching it as they walked.

Trevor slanted him a sidelong glance. "Yeah. Me, too."

He tried to sound indifferent about it, but Bob knew him too well not to pick up on the sarcasm.

"So, what happened?"

"She had a meeting at the studio," Trevor said. "At least that's what she said."

Bob frowned. "You sound like you don't believe her."

Trevor shrugged. "There wasn't anything about a meeting on her calendar. I checked."

He was embarrassed to even admit it, but something about Addison had been off. Like she hadn't been able to get away from his fast enough. He'd pulled up her calendar on her computer without even realizing what he'd been doing.

"Maybe she didn't write it on her computer," Bob said. "Maybe she put it on her BlackBerry."

When Trevor didn't say anything, his friend sighed.

"You don't honestly think she's playing you, do you?" the other man asked.

"I don't know what to think."

Bob swore under his breath. "Man, you've been in Hollywood too long. You can't even recognize when a woman is genuinely in love with you."

Trevor stopped walking to look at his friend in astonishment. "In love with me? What the hell gives you that idea?'

Bob stopped, too. "Damn, Trevor, anyone can see it. Addison's so into you, she barely knows anyone else is in the room when you're there."

Trevor snorted. "I doubt that." He gestured to the football. "We going to throw that thing around, or what?"

Bob looked like he wanted to talk about Addison some more, but after a moment, he shook his head. "Whatever."

He and Bob didn't talk while they tossed the football back and forth, which suited Trevor just fine. He was too busy having a silent conversation with himself. Was Bob right? Did Addison have feelings for him? Sometimes, he thought she did, but the way she'd acted earlier made him doubt everything he knew or felt. His gut told him she was hiding something from him — something big.

When he mentioned it to Bob as they were driving back to the house a little while later, his friend frowned.

"You're not going to let this go, are you?"

"You're the one who insists she has feelings for me," Trevor said. "I'm just trying to figure out what's up with her."

Bob let out a sigh. "Look, Addison definitely has some stuff she needs to talk to you about. And before you ask, no, I'm not going to tell you what it is. It's her secret to tell. But take my word for it, she has feelings for you. Just like you have feelings for her."

Trevor scowled, but didn't say anything. Was he that transparent? Some actor he was.

Right now, he didn't care if Bob knew he liked Addison — well, maybe more than liked her — he was more interested in the secret she was keeping from him. A secret she'd obviously confided in Bob about. He scowled again.

To his relief, Addison's car was parked out front when he and Bob got home, and he was suddenly impatient as his friend drove around back to park in the garage. As soon as he went inside, he was going to sit her down and have a long talk with her. Of course, if he wanted her to confide in him, then that meant he'd have to open up, too. After confessing his love for women in front of a camera for years, doing it for real should be a piece of cake, but it scared the hell out of him. Especially since he didn't know if Addison felt the same way.

When he and Bob walked inside, though, it was to see Addison's car speeding down the driveway. Now, where the hell was she going?

"Was that Addison's car I just saw leaving?" Trevor asked Murray.

His manager was standing in the kitchen with a frown on his face.

"I'm afraid to say that it was." The man frowned. "I don't know how to tell you this, Trevor, especially since I know you were just getting used to having her as your new assistant, but Addison just quit."

Trevor's eyes went wide. "What?" he and Bob said in unison.

"I know," Murray said. "It surprised me, too. She came in a few minutes ago and said she found another job. She said working for you was too stressful."

Trevor was so stunned he couldn't say anything. Even if he could have made his mouth move, he wouldn't have known what to say. A few minutes earlier, he'd been ready to believe that Addison cared about him. How could he have been so wrong?

"Listen, Trevor," Murray said. "I have some other business I have to take care of. I'll see you later. Then we'll work on getting you a new assistant."

Trevor nodded automatically. He pulled a chair out from the table and sank down into it.

"So much for Addison being in love with me," he said bitterly. "I can't believe she'd just up and leave without saying goodbye. She might not give a damn about me, but I know she cared about you, Maribel and Leo. I would have at least expected her to say something to you guys before she left."

"Me, too," Bob said. "Something's not right here. Hold on a second. I'm going to check something out."

Trevor started to ask his friend where he was going, but the other man had already left the kitchen. A moment later, he heard Bob run upstairs. When he came back a few minutes later, he was frowning.

"I was right. Something is definitely off here," he said "Addison didn't take any of her stuff, not even the new dress you brought her for the Oscar. No woman walks out without taking a five-thousand-dollar dress, no matter how stressful the job is."

Trevor's eyes narrowed. He wasn't exactly clued-in when it came to women, but he had to admit Bob had a point. If he'd been thinking straight, he would have figured it out himself. "I agree with you about that. But then where the hell did she go?"

Leo walked in before Bob could offer a theory. He opened the fridge and grabbed a bottle of soda, giving Bob a curious look as he unscrewed the cap. "I thought you were with Addison."

Trevor exchanged looks with Bob.

"Why would Bob be with Addison?" he asked.

Leo took a swallow of cola. "I don't know. She was in the car with somebody big and I figured it must be Bob."

Trevor frowned. "She left with someone?"

"Yeah," Leo said. "An SUV sped out right behind them, too."

Trevor felt his a knot form in the pit of his stomach. He quickly told Leo what Murray had said about Addison quitting. Leo looked as surprised as he and Bob had been.

"She didn't say anything to you about leaving, did she?" Trevor asked.

Leo asked. "No. She came into the garage a couple of hours ago and asked for some directions to the industrial part of town, but she didn't say anything about leaving."

Trevor's brow furrowed. "The industrial part of town? Why would she want to go there?"

"She didn't say. She just said she had to look into something."

"Do you remember the address?" Trevor asked.

Leo nodded, rattling it off. Trevor's frown deepened. He'd always been good at remembering things and addresses were no exception.

"I know that place," he said. Pulling out his BlackBerry, he brought up the website for Total Empire Investment and Trust. "That's the address of my bank."

Bob lifted a brow. "Your bank is in the industrial section? You sure?"

"I'm sure."

"That never struck you as strange?"

"I never realized it was the industrial section. Murray always took care of that stuff."

Bob let out a breath. "I don't think Addison trusts Murray quite as much as you do. No wonder she wanted to go check it out."

"Do you think we should we call the cops?" Leo asked.

Trevor considered it, then shook his head. What would they tell them? "Later. Right now, I want to get out to that warehouse and see what the hell is going on."

* * *

Murray's thugs took Addison to the same warehouse she'd been to earlier. She struggled the minute one of the men dragged her out of the car, but the brute only picked her up and tossed her over his shoulder, then carried her inside. Once there, he took her to a small office and dumped her in a straight-backed chair. Before she could even try to get to her feet, he'd tied her hands behind her back and put a piece of duct tape over her mouth. She glared at him, but her just gave her an amused look and left to go wait for Murray in the main part of the building along with his partner.

How long would it take for Murray to get there? What would he tell Trevor when she didn't come back?

Tears filled her eyes and she blinked them away. God, how she wished she'd spent the day with Trevor liked he'd wanted to instead of playing Nancy Drew. Now, not only would he never know Murray was stealing from him, but he'd never know she was in love with him, either. If she'd just confided in him about her suspicions regarding Total Empire Investment and Trust, then none of this would have happened.

Out in the other room, a door opened, then closed. She tensed at the sound of Murray's voice. He was talking to his goons in low tones, so she couldn't really hear what he was saying, but she thought she heard Trevor's name.

A few minutes later, Murray walked in, his thugs at his heels. She glowered at them, but the fury in her gaze had little effect on either Murray or the men with him.

He glanced at the man on his right. She didn't know if he was the one who had tied her up or not. As far as she was concerned, the assholes were interchangeable.

"Take off the tape," Murray instructed.

The man crossed the room in two strides, ripping the tape off her mouth so fast she was sure he must have taken some skin with it. Addison winced, but wouldn't give him the satisfaction of crying out. Instead, she glared up at Murray.

"You won't get away with this," she told him. "Trevor will wonder what happened to me when I don't come home."

Murray snickered. "Trevor thinks you quit. I told him you said the job was too stressful."

Addison blinked. "He won't believe you." He couldn't. Not after making love last night.

"Trevor believes anything I tell him. He'd just a farm boy. That's why it's so easy to dupe him out of his money." Murray folded his arms. "I'm going to keep this simple. Who do you work for, how much do you know, and who have you told?"

"I told you. I work for Trevor, just like you do."

Murray glanced at the man who had taken off the tape, then turned his gaze back to her.

"Bruno here likes making people talk, and the methods he uses aren't always very nice. In fact, they're extremely painful. So, if you don't want to experience those methods firsthand then you'd better start talking."

Beside Murray, Bruno smiled menacingly, and Addison swallowed hard.

"Okay," she said softly. "I-I wasn't lying when I said I work for Trevor. But I'm not his personal assistant. I'm a private investigator he hired to find out where his money was disappearing to."

She didn't exactly look like a private investigator, so she didn't know if Murray would believe it or not, but it was the only thing she could come up with. If she kept saying she was nothing more than a personal assistant, he would turn her over to Bruno. Besides, if he believed she was a PI, then he might think she'd told someone what she knew and therefore be more reluctant to kill her. It had worked in one of Trevor's movies when he'd convinced the bad guys he was a private investigator who'd stumbled on them by accident instead of the FBI agent he really was. But that was a movie and this was real life. Murray probably wouldn't believe her, especially if he'd seen the movie, too.

But either Murray hadn't seen the movie or she was a better liar than she thought, because gave Bruno a sidelong glance.

"Check her purse," he said.

Addison didn't know what he expected to find in it — if she had a gun, she would have tried to use it — but she watched as Bruno grabbed her purse from the table and dumped out the contents. There wasn't much in it other than her wallet, keys and makeup. And the radio Leo had given her to use in case she and Trevor ever got into trouble. This certainly qualified as trouble. Unfortunately, the radio wouldn't do her much good. Or maybe it would. Her pulse quickened as she realized she'd left it switched to monitor mode. She didn't know what kind of range the radio had, but if by some chance Bob had his own radio nearby, then he'd be able to hear what was going on. For all the good it would do. Even if Trevor and Bob realized she'd been kidnapped, they'd have no way of knowing where she was. Her heart sank at that.

Murray mustn't have liked what he saw on the table because he swore under his breath. "I didn't think Trevor was bright enough to notice I was stealing from him, but apparently I was wrong."

Addison's eyes narrowed. How dare he think Trevor was stupid. "Of course he's on to you. He suspected it was you for a long time. He just wanted me to get proof."

Murray's mouth tightened. "Really? That's too bad. Now I'll have to take care of him, too."

Addison's heart seized in her chest as she realized her mistake. If she'd just kept her mouth shut, Trevor wouldn't be in danger. But it was too late to take it back.

"I had a good thing going, too," Murray continued. "But you have to know when to cut bait and head for deeper water. It was time to take our money and move on anyway. I've never played one con for this long, so I'm ready for something else."

She looked at him incredulously. "You've been Trevor's manager for years. Are you saying you've been conning him all along?"

Murray smirked. "I'm not sure if you know this, but there's not much difference between a manager and a con man. They both involve blowing sunshine up the asses of a lot of gullible people. I'd only planned to suck a few bucks out of Trevor when I first convinced him that I could manage his career. Hell, back then he only had a few bucks. But what do you know, he hit it big. So, I went along for the ride. And on the way, I got money out of a few more stars, too."

Addison couldn't believe it. Being a con man was almost worse than being a greedy manager out for what he could get. Then again, people who lived in glass houses shouldn't throw stones. As much as she hated to admit it, she was no better than Murray. Maybe her crime wasn't as egregious, but she had conned Trevor, too.

Murray turned to the two men. "Get rid of her. And dump her body somewhere it won't be found."

Bruno and his counterpart looked only too pleased to carry out the order. Addison's heart began to pound. She struggled against the ropes binding her to the chair, but it did no good. All she could do was sit there and watch as the two men approached her.

The man with Bruno eyed her up and down. "You're cute. Too bad we can't have a little fun with you first."

"Don't be an idiot, Carlos," Murray said. "We have to be at the dock by four and we still have to get rid of Trevor Braden. You can have all the women you want when we get to Mexico."

Neither man looked pleased at that, but they must have seen Murray's point because Bruno pulled out a gun.

Even though she knew it would do no good, Addison opened her mouth to scream when she heard a loud noise from the main part of the warehouse. Bruno froze.

Murray frowned and motioned with his head. "You two go check it out. I'll stay here with her."

Bruno immediately headed for the door. Carlos reached behind his back for the gun he had tucked in his waistband, then followed him out. Hoping the noise meant someone else was in the warehouse, Addison drew in a breath to scream, but Murray slapped the piece of tape over her mouth again before she could make a sound.

Addison sat there tensely, trying to hear what was going on with Bruno and Carlos, but all she heard was the sound of her own heart pounding. In a minute, the two men would come back and kill her. She should have been terrified, and yet she was more afraid for Trevor then she was for herself. She had gotten into this mess by foolishly snooping around. Trevor, however, would never know what hit him. The thought brought tears to her eyes.

From outside, there came a loud crash, then a strangled shout. Addison jumped.

"What the hell?" Murray muttered.

He threw her a quick glance, then took a gun from inside his jacket and crossed the room to the door. The moment he stepped outside the office, a blur went streaking past the doorway, hitting him square in the chest and knocking him off his feet.

Addison's eyes went wide at the sight of dark hair and big, broad shoulders. Trevor!

She screamed against the tape covering her mouth, trying to warn him that Murray had a gun, but the sound was muffled. Not that Trevor would have been able to hear her anyway because the men rolled across the floor and out of sight. Dammit!

She struggled against the ropes again, but it was just as futile as it had been before. Terrified for Trevor and desperate to see what was going on, she tried to scoot the chair closer to the door and almost ended up tipping it over. She slid the chair across the floor again, more carefully this time, only to freeze when she heard a gunshot. Her heart stopped. Trevor. Oh dear God, no.

She held her breath as footsteps hurried toward the room, expecting to see Murray. But it was Trevor. All six-foot-four glorious inches of him! Fresh tears streamed down her face, this time from joy. He was still alive!

Dropping to his knee in front of her, Trevor carefully pulled off the tape, then covered her mouth with his in a kiss that left her breathless by the time he pulled away.

"Murray had two men with him," she said urgently. "We have to get out of here."

"Bob already took care of them." He cupped her cheek, his eyes intent as they studied her face. "God, Addison, I thought you were dead. I've never been so scared in my life."

"Me, either," she admitted softly. "I thought Murray was going to kill you." She swallowed hard. "Is he...?"

"Dead? Yeah, I think so. I didn't really check. We fought over the gun and it went off. He can't hurt us anymore." Trevor leaned forward to kiss her again. "Let me untie you."

The moment Addison was free, he pulled her to her feet and into his arms, hugging her tightly. She wrapped her arms around him just as tightly. She never wanted to let him go, and probably wouldn't have, at least for the next hour or two, if Bob hadn't come in. Even then, she was reluctant to Trevor get too far away and only lifted her head from his chest so she could look at the other man. Trevor didn't seem to mind, though.

Bob grinned at her. "I see Trevor saved the day."

Addison smiled, shifting her gaze to look up at her handsome employer. "Yes, he did. Just like in the movies."

Now that Murray was no longer a danger, and she and Trevor were safe, she finally realized how dramatic — and heroic — his rescue had been. Trevor, however, seemed embarrassed.

130

"I didn't do all that much. If Murray's gun hadn't gone off, I'd probably still be fighting with him," he insisted. "Bob had to deal with the real thugs." He looked at his bodyguard. "Where are they, anyway?"

"They were a couple of cupcakes. I left them tied up out there," Bob said. "The police are on their way."

Trevor nodded, then looked down at her. He reached out to smooth her hair back from her face. "Leo said you came here earlier and after hearing the address, I figured out it belonged to the investment company. Or at least this is supposed to be their address. Then we heard Murray talking over your radio and realized he was a con man. What I don't understand is how you figured it all out when we never did."

She quickly told him about recognizing Bill Worthington from the bank's website and that he'd mentioned Murray. "Bill called Murray to have it out with him, and Murray decided he had to get rid of me because I knew too much." Her brow furrowed as something occurred to her. "How did you know to come to the warehouse? More importantly, how did you even know to come looking for me? Murray said he told you I'd quit."

Trevor's jaw tightened. "I didn't believe him, especially after Leo said he saw you leaving with a couple of guys. I figured there was something suspicious going on here and took a chance whoever kidnapped you would bring you here. I didn't know for sure Murray was involved until we got close enough to pick up the radio signal. When we heard him threatening you, I knew we had to move. We couldn't wait for the cops."

She shuddered as much from the reminder of Murray's threats as from the memory of Trevor fighting with the man. Trevor must have seen her reaction because he hugged her close again. In the distance, she could heard sirens approaching. Before either of them could say anything more, Leo came in, along with half a dozen uniformed cops.

Any hope Addison had of forgetting the nightmare they'd just lived through and going back to Trevor's place disappeared when the police started taking their statements. Trevor might be a well-known movie star, but there still was a dead body to explain, plus two beaten-up men who wouldn't be talking anytime soon, thanks to Bob. When Addison explained about the investment trust scam, saying Murray had hinted he might have duped other Hollywood stars as well, higher ranking police officers showed up and insisted she, Trevor, Bob and Leo go over their stories again.

As if that weren't enough, the press had somehow gotten wind of Trevor's involvement, which meant it wasn't long before the place was crawling with reporters. There were even news helicopters hovering above the building.

By the time the cops were done with them, it was nearly midnight. Addison expected to be assaulted by paparazzi the moment she and Trevor left the warehouse, but the police managed to keep the crowd behind the yellow crime scene tape. Bob was able to hurry her and Trevor to the limo without incident, though the hundreds of flashbulbs nearly blinded her.

To her relief, the cops gave them an escort home, which was a good thing because there were more reporters waiting outside the mansion. Thanks goodness Trevor had a gate with guards manning it, otherwise they would have been accosted the minute they got home.

Addison wasn't surprised to see Maribel glued to the huge plasma television in the living room, watching the news. The cook jumped up from the couch to hug each of them in turn as soon as they walked into the house. Despite having seen everything on TV, Maribel wanted to know the

132

full story and wouldn't let them go to bed until they recounted every detail.

"I never liked that Murray from the minute Trevor hired him," Maribel said when they'd finished. She looked at Trevor. "I do hope you're giving Addison a raise for figuring out what a thieving bastard he was."

Addison shook her head. "That's not necessary. I was only doing my job."

"Nonsense," the other woman insisted. "You went above and beyond, and you deserve a raise."

Addison opened her mouth to protest again, but Trevor slipped his arm around her.

"Maribel's right. You do deserve a raise." He leaned closer, putting his mouth to her ear. "Among other things."

The promise in his whisper sent a delightful little shiver through Addison. Even though she was sure the others hadn't heard what Trevor said, she still blushed. Maribel, Bob and Leo must have taken that as their cue to leave because a little while afterward, they all said good night.

"You must be worn out," Trevor said when they were alone.

"I am a little tired," she admitted.

"Then we should get you into bed."

Her pussy purred at his words and she had bite her lip to stifle a moan. She needed to get hold of herself. Just because she and Trevor had slept together the night before that didn't mean he intended for her to spend tonight there, too. Which was why she reluctantly headed for her room when they got upstairs.

"Where are you going?" Trevor asked.

She turned to see him regarding her curiously. "To bed."

His mouth edged up. "My room is this way."

Addison's heart did a little backflip as she took Trevor's outstretched hand and let him lead her down the hallway to his bedroom. Once inside, he closed the door, then pulled her into his arms for a long, intoxicating kiss that had her clinging to his shoulders by the time he lifted his head.

He took her face in both his hands, his dark eyes full of emotion as he gazed down at her. "You have no idea how terrified I was tonight. When I heard those bastards talk about hurting you, I wanted to tear them apart."

She let out a shudder. "When I think what would have happened if you'd believed Murray when he told you I quit..."

"I knew you wouldn't just leave without saying anything." He wrapped his arms around her, hugging her close. "Why did you run out to that warehouse by yourself anyway? Why didn't you just tell me what your suspicions were?"

"I didn't want you thinking I was snooping in your business," she said in a soft voice.

He stepped back, holding her at arm's length with gentle hands. "You're my assistant, Addison. My business is your business."

"I know. It's just that I wanted to be sure about Murray before I said anything." She looped her arms around Trevor's neck. "Enough about him and what happened tonight. I'd rather talk about whatever it was you were referring to downstairs. You know, the other thing you promised you'd give me in addition to a raise."

"Oh, that." He grinned. "I was going to wait until tomorrow when we both weren't so tired, but it's probably better if I give it to you now."

Heat pooled between her thighs and settled there as Trevor took her hand and led her over to the bed. Instead

134

of kissing her again or even taking off her clothes, he sat down and pulled her over his lap.

Startled, she jerked her head around to look at him over her shoulder. "What are you doing?"

He placed his hand on the small of her back. "I'd think that after being in this position numerous times over the past week you'd know what I'm going to do."

Her eyes went wide. "You're going to spank me?"

His mouth quirked. "Of course. What did you think I was talking about downstairs?"

"That you were going to make love to me until I couldn't see straight!"

"I am," he said. "After I redden your bottom."

"But—"

He ran other hand over her skirt, giving her ass a squeeze. "How else am I going to make sure you'll never do anything as crazy or as dangerous as you did tonight again?"

"Because I promise I won't."

He was silent for a moment, as if considering that. "I don't know. How do I know you're being honest and not just telling me what I want to hear?"

"Because I would never do that." She sighed. "Besides, it's not like your next manger is going to swindle you, too, so it isn't very likely I'll do anything that dangerous again."

"Probably not," he agreed. "I think I'll spank you anyway, just to be on the safe side."

Addison opened her mouth to protest again, then closed it. Why was she trying to talk him out of spanking her when she got so aroused by it? Her pussy was already quivering at the thought as it was. Deciding to simply give in and enjoy it, she turned around and settled into a comfortable position.

Trevor squeezed her ass again. His hand was warm through the thin material of her skirt and she caught her breath. She waited breathlessly for him to start smacking her bottom, but instead he gently caressed her upturned cheeks. She bit her lip to stifle a moan.

All at once, he stopped what he was doing and lifted his hand, bringing it down on her right cheek with a firm smack. Addison's gasp was quickly followed by a squeal as his hand immediately connected with her other cheek. She barely had time to catch her breath before he followed it up with another, falling into that same easy rhythm he had the other times he'd spanked her. He smacked first one cheek, then the other until her entire bottom was warm and tingling. Only then did he stop, and that was only so he could push up her skirt.

Addison moaned as he gave her ass a firm squeeze. Rather than rub the sting from her cheeks like she hoped he would, though, he immediately went back to spanking her again. Heat spread across he derriere and she squirmed on his lap. Her wiggling made her skimpy panties ride up to expose more of her ass cheeks, and she squealed each time his hand connected with her bare skin.

Then, just as quickly as the spanking had started, it stopped. She looked over her shoulder at Trevor, wondering if he was done, but he gave her a lazy grin. Hooking his fingers in the waistband of her panties, he slowly slid them down to mid-thigh, then lightly ran his fingers up her legs. She caught her lower lip between her teeth, her heart pounding as she waited for him to slip his hand between them and touch her pussy. But instead, he lifted his hand and smacked her hard on the bare ass.

She squealed, wiggling on his lap in rhythm with the spanks as he moved from one cheek to the other. Between her legs, her pussy tingled like crazy and it was all she could do not to touch herself. And yet, she knew that resisting the urge would only make her orgasm that much more powerful when she had it.

The spanking felt so amazing that when Trevor stopped, she almost protested, but then he bent and pressed his lips to her red-hot ass. She moaned as the stubble on his jaw brushed her sensitive skin. Suddenly the tingling in her pussy turned into an insistent throb she couldn't deny any longer.

She looked at him over her shoulder. "Touch me. Please."

Trevor lifted his head, his gaze meeting her. His was hot and hungry and it sent shivers of desire through her. Mouth curving into a sinfully sexy smile, he slipped his hand between her legs and ran his fingers along her slick folds. She cooed as he found her clit and made little, lazy circles around it.

Instead of touching her until she came, though, he slid his fingers up and down her slit before dipping inside her wetness. Even then, he teased her, wiggling his finger back and forth, then pulling out. She started to beg him to continue but he was already standing her up and getting to his feet. Cupping her freshly spanked ass cheeks in both hands, he pulled her close and kissed her.

His mouth was possessive, his tongue plunging into her mouth to tangle urgently with hers, and she buried her hands in his dark hair, kissing him back just as passionately. His hard cock pressed up against her through the material of his jeans, letting her know how much he wanted her.

Trevor's hands glided over her hips and up her abdomen to cup her breasts through her top. Her nipples tightened in response to his touch, straining at the thin material, and she sighed against his mouth as he rubbed his thumbs over their sensitive tips.

Murmuring something unintelligible against her mouth, he broke the kiss to pull her top over her head. He made quick work of her bra as well, sending it sailing across the room. He cupped her breasts in his hands again, bending to suck one rosy red peak in his mouth even as he took the other between his forefinger and thumb and gave it a squeeze.

Addison arched against him, clutching his broad shoulders as he swirled his tongue around first one nipple, then the other until they were both wet and tingling.

Groaning, he lifted his head and turned her around so that she was facing the bed. Placing his hand on her back, he urged her forward until she was leaning over it. Addison thought it was so he could spank her again, but after unzipping her skirt and pulling her panties the rest of the way down, he dropped to his knees behind her, then cupping her ass, spread her wide so he could bury his face in her pussy.

Addison caught her breath. She'd never had a guy give her oral sex in this position before. She automatically arched her back, sighing as Trevor ran his tongue along the slick folds of her pussy. She leaned further forward and thrust her ass even higher in the air, hoping his magical tongue would find its way to her clit. He must have been able to read her body language because a moment later she felt his velvety tongue on her plump, little nub.

She moaned, spreading her legs even more as he began making slow circles round and round the sensitive flesh. In this position, she was even more sensitive than usual and when he ran his tongue along her pussy and dipped it inside, she thought she might actually come just from that. Before she could find out, however, he moved back up to her clit again.

Instead of making slow, languorous circles on the plump flesh

like before, he flicked his tongue over her clit once, then twice, before closing his mouth over the sensitive bud and gently sucking on it. Addison gasped, sure what he was doing was going to send her tumbling over the edge, but Trevor was obviously determined to tease her because he went back to making circular motions on her clit with his tongue. Damn, he knew how to get her hot and bothered!

Addison closed her eyes, gyrating her hips in time with his tongue and letting herself get lost in how good it felt. It was like every nerve in her body was concentrated inside her clit.

All at once, her breath started coming in quick, little pant as she got closer and closer to climax. The sensation was so intense, she was barely even aware of what Trevor was doing as he lapped her clit with his tongue.

Her orgasm swept over her with the force of a tidal wave, and she dug her fingers into the bedding, her screams echoing through the house as Trevor coaxed every trace of pleasure from her body.

Afterward, all she could do was lie there draped over the bed. Behind her, Trevor pressed a tender kiss to her still-tingling ass. She sighed, barely aware of him getting to his feet. When she heard him unbuckle his belt and push down his jeans, she wondered if she should push herself up from the bed and turn around, but then she felt Trevor's hands on her hips. Her breath hitched. He was going to take her from behind. She'd had sex in that position before, of course, but there was something so much hotter about doing it like that after she'd just been spanked. She blushed as she imagined how she must look, bent over the bed, her freshly-spanked red ass on display.

Addison waited breathlessly for him to enter her, but instead Trevor teased her by running the head of his cock up and down her wetness. She moaned. While what he was doing felt delicious, she wanted more.

"Stop teasing me. I need you inside me," she demanded. "Now!"

She was half afraid Trevor might tease her anyway, but to her relief he tightened his grip on her hips and slid his hard length into her pussy in one smooth thrust.

For a moment, he stayed like that, his cock nestled deep inside of her and Addison caught her lower lip between her teeth, her body shuddering at the feel of his cock pulsating inside her. Then he slowly began to pump in and out with agonizing slowness.

She rocked back against him. "Harder!"

Trevor obeyed. Tightening his hold on her, he began to
move his cock in and out of her faster and faster. The force of his thrusts shoved her against the bed and she grasped hold of the sheets so that she could push back.

"Yes," she cried. "Just like that. Harder! Fuck me harder!"

He did.

She knew from the deep, husky groans he was making that his orgasm was only moments away, and she held her own back, wanting to come with him. When he finally exploded inside her with a release of cum so hot she swore she could feel it, she let herself go, and the climax that swept her away was more powerful than any she'd ever had in her life.

Sliding out, Trevor took her hand and together, they crawled into bed. Addison snuggled up to him, her arm thrown across his chest, her head pillowed on his shoulder. She didn't know where this thing with Trevor was going, if anywhere, but right then she didn't care. She had never been happier. To think, she'd almost left after her first day on the job simply because he'd put her over his knee and spanked her. Now, she couldn't wait for him to spank her again.

While the thought made her smile, it also made her realize if ever did want this thing with Trevor to go somewhere, she was going to have to come clean with him,

140

just like she promised herself she would. Now wasn't the time, though. They were both so exhausted they could barely keep their eyes open. She would tell him everything first thing in the morning.

Chapter Eight

Addison didn't know what time it was when the phone beside the bed rang. She knew it had to be early because the sun wasn't up yet. She snuggled against Trevor's chest, hoping the darn thing would stop if they ignored it. No such luck.

Mumbling something under his breath she couldn't make out, Trevor fumbled for the phone and held it to his ear.

"This better be important," he growled.

Her lips curved at the unconventional greeting. Fortunately, only a handful of people had his private number, and none of them would be insulted by the curt words.

"What?" He frowned into the phone. "No, I'll talk to them. Just give me time to get some clothes on."

He dropped the phone back in its cradle. "Dammit."

Addison pushed herself up on her elbow. "What is it?"

He wiped his hand down his face. "That was Bob. There are at least fifty reporters at the front gate looking for an interview."

Her brow furrowed. Trevor had already planned to do a few intimate interviews in the living room before the premiere anyway, then head over to the theater before everyone else got there so he wouldn't have to deal with the whole red carpet craziness. After last night they should have expected that plan would get shot to hell.

"At this time in the morning?" she asked.

"I guess they all wanted to be the first to get the scoop."

Since none of them had been able to get it last night. "Do you want me to get rid of them for you?"

Trevor sighed. "No. I'll talk to them." He reached up to push her long hair back from her face. "I'd planned on keeping you in bed all day and making love to every inch of your beautiful body. Instead, I have to ask you to go back to playing my assistant and deal with this chaos."

She smiled. "Dealing with chaos is my job, remember? Though I'd much rather stay in bed and let you make love to me. If we're lucky, the reporters will be in and out, and you'll be done in time for us to have time for a quickie before we have to leave for the premiere."

He pulled her down for a long, lingering kiss. "And if we don't, we can always do it in the limo on the way there."

The image made her pussy quiver, and it was all she could do to drag herself out of bed. As she hurried downstairs a little while later, it occurred to her that she hadn't gotten a chance to talk to Trevor about who she really was. She sighed. It looked like coming clean would have to wait — again.

Taking the reporters' names and setting up a schedule would have been a lot easier if they hadn't kept trying to interview her while she did it. They seemed just as interested in her role in last night's adventures as they were in Trevor. Maybe more interested. She did her best to downplay her part in what had happened at the warehouse, but she wasn't sure they bought it. When they continued to press her about it, she merely smiled and politely got them back on task.

In the interest of fairness, she gave the first slots to the reporters who had already been scheduled to meet with Trevor. Everyone else got a ten-minute slot to get their interview in. No cameras in the house, just recorders and notepads. There was a lot of grumbling about that little stipulation, but with Bob there to back her up, she stood her ground.

As usual, Trevor amazed her. He treated every reporter who interviewed him as if they were an old friend and answered each question as if he hadn't heard it a hundred times before. Though they asked about his new movie, they were more eager to hear about Murray and his goons trying to kill her and Trevor. While Trevor was as open as he could be about the previous evening's events, he refrained from giving any of them too many details, saying the police were still conducting their investigation.

"I really didn't do much," he told the female reporter who had most recently asked the question. "My assistant Addison was the one who figured out my manager was embezzling, and my bodyguard Bob was the one who saved everyone's life."

Addison wanted to say that wasn't true, that Trevor had been the real hero, but even if she had corrected him, she knew he wouldn't take the credit anyway.

The dark-haired woman gave Addison an appraising look before turning her attention back to Trevor. "There's some speculation out there that Addison is more than just your assistant."

Addison blushed at the question, sure Trevor must be as uncomfortable with it as she was. Where had the woman heard a rumor like that?

"I don't know what you've heard, Rowena," Trevor said, "but if you're asking if Addison is important to me, the answer is yes." He glanced at Addison, giving her a heart-stopping grin. "She's very important to me."

Addison's breath hitched at the emotion in his dark eyes. She tried not to read too much into his words, but when he looked at her like that it was impossible not to. Which made it very difficult to concentrate on anything else for the rest of the day. Thankfully, there was only one more interview after Rowena, so she didn't have to expend too much energy thinking about anything else.

By the time the last reporter left, she and Trevor had to hurry upstairs to get ready to the premiere. While it was fun to secretly pretend she was Trevor's date for the event as she twirled in front of the full-length mirror dressed in the outrageously expensive gown he'd bought for her, she was back in personal-assistant mode when she hurried downstairs. Until she saw Trevor in his tux. The man wasn't just handsome; he was sex-on-a-stick yummy.

He was talking to Bob when she came down, but he stopped mid-sentence when he saw her. His eyes caressed every inch of her body, lingering on every curve, and she felt herself blush.

"Addison," he breathed. "You look absolutely beautiful."

"Thank you." She ran her suddenly damp hands down the front of the exquisite black evening gown with a flirtatious little smile. "You don't look so bad yourself."

Trevor chuckled, the sound deep and sexy. He glanced at Bob. "Tell Leo we're ready to leave, would you?"

Bob gave her a wink. "Sure thing."

Trevor didn't even wait for the Bob to leave before he bent is head to kiss her. "I know that's going to wreak havoc on your lipstick, but I couldn't wait until after the premiere to do that."

She laughed and would have told him she didn't care what it did to her lipstick as long as he kept kissing her, but he closed his mouth over hers again. He didn't lift his head until Bob let out a discreet cough from the doorway, and by then she was breathless. She didn't know how she was going to wait all those hours until the premiere was over and she could get him alone.

Addison put on more lipstick in the car, but not until they were near the theater, just in case Trevor wanted to kiss her some more. Which he did. Several times.

As she dropped the tube of lipstick in her evening bag, she leaned forward to remind Leo to drop her off at the side entrance before taking Trevor around to the red carpet.

"No need, Leo," Trevor said. "Addison isn't going in the side entrance."

She looked at him in confusion. "I'm not?"

"No." He reached out to push back a stray strand of hair that had escaped from her elaborate updo. "You're walking down the red carpet with me."

Her eyes went wide. "But..."

"No buts." His mouth twitched. "Or I'll think you don't want to be seen with me."

"Don't want to be seen with you?" She almost laughed. "Are you sure you want to be seen with me? Trevor, if I walk up the red carpet with you, people are going to think we're a couple."

"So? We are a couple. Aren't we?"

"Well, yes, but I'm your personal assistant."

"You're way more than that to me, Addison Mattingly," he said. "It's time the rest of the world knows it."

Between Trevor announcing their relationship and the prospect of walking down the red carpet, Addison's heart was beating so fast by the time the limo rolled to a stop in front of the theater she thought she might pass out. She opened her mouth to tell Trevor, but he'd already stepped out of the limo and extended his hand to her. Outside the car, the applause was thunderous. Taking a deep breath, she put her hand in his and stepped out onto the curb.

Having seen every premiere of every one of Trevor's movies on television, she'd expected the crowd of screaming fans to be huge, but it was much bigger than it looked on TV. The flashbulbs on the cameras were brighter, too, and as Trevor put his arm around her, she felt every bit the celebrity. Not to mention the luckiest woman in the world. It was like being in her own version of Cinderella.

Walking down the red carpet was only half of it, though. Getting interviewed was the other half, and every entertainment reporter along the way stopped her and Trevor. Like the ones who'd come to the mansion, they were more interested in whether Addison and Trevor were an item. He smiled and gave the same answer he had before, saying she was very important to him.

As they moved on to the next reporter, the one who'd just finished interviewing them smiled into the camera. "There you have it, folks. Trevor Bradon is finally off the market. And something tells me, it might be for good this time."

Addison knew it was nothing more than a reporter trying to sensationalize the story, but the idea of a future with Trevor made her warm all over.

They stepped into the lobby amid more applause, this time from producers, directors and fellow actors. As excited as she was to be beside Trevor, it was nothing compared to how she felt when he tightened his arm around her waist and pulled her a little closer as the crowd surrounded them. It was as if he was announcing to the world that they really were a couple.

Addison thought they would go directly into the theater to watch the movie, but instead they mingled in the lobby enjoying champagne and hors d' oeuvres. She was nibbling on a canapé when the film's producer and director went up to the dais to address the audience.

"It wouldn't be right to stand up here and not mention last night's adventures," the director finished, giving the crowd a big smile. "How many of you knew Trevor was a real-life action-adventure hero? Fighting three men and rescuing his beautiful assistant from certain death. I couldn't have scripted it better myself."

Beside her, Trevor flushed beneath his tan, clearly embarrassed by the praise and the round of applause that went with it. Addison stopped clapping to go up on tiptoe and kiss him on the cheek even as a chorus of "speech, speech, speech," echoed around them.

Chuckling, Trevor took her hand and headed for the dais, taking Addison with him. She tried to hang back, but he wouldn't let her. She blushingly followed, standing beside him as he spoke. Once again, he downplayed his role in the previous night's events. At that, her shyness immediately disappeared. Before she even realized what she was doing, she leaned forward and commandeered the microphone.

"Trevor is just being modest. If it weren't for him, his manager and the thugs who worked for him would have killed me, so don't let him tell you any differently. He truly is a real-life action-adventure hero." She gave him a smile. "Mine."

That made Trevor's face color again, but the audience clearly approved because they applauded again, this time even louder.

"I thought we put together a pretty good film." The director laughed as he leaned in to take the microphone again. "But I'm not sure how it's going to compete with last night."

It turned out the director was being modest, too. The movie was wonderful and everyone enjoyed it, most especially Addison, who got to sit there with Trevor's arm around her the whole time. When they went back into the lobby afterward, more than one person came over to congratulate Trevor and tell him he had a huge hit on his hands. Addison agreed.

The crowd outside the theater hadn't gotten any smaller by the time they left, and she and Trevor were treated to more applause as Bob escorted them to the limo.

The moment they were alone, Trevor pulled her into his arms for a long, intoxicating kiss. "I've wanted to do that for hours."

She moaned. "You have no idea how much I wanted you to."

He kissed her again. "Hold that thought."

She lifted a questioning brow, but Trevor only leaned forward in his seat.

"Take the long way home, Leo."

"Will do."

As Trevor put up the privacy divider, Addison saw Leo and Bob exchange grins, and she couldn't help but blush.

Trevor gave her a sexy grin. "Now, where were we?"

She smiled. "You were kissing me."

His grin broadened. "I was, wasn't I?"

He pulled her into his arms, one hand pulling the pins from her hair, the other cupping her breast through the silky material of her gown. Her nipple hardened to a stiff peak at his touch, and she sighed against his mouth. If they weren't in the back of his limo, she'd have her gown off and be all over him.

Apparently, Trevor didn't seem to care where they were because he slid straps of her dress over her shoulders and down her arms until her bare breasts were exposed.

She blushed and immediately covered herself with her arms. "What about Bob and Leo?"

"What about them?"

"Won't they hear?"

His mouth twitched. "Not if we're quiet."

She could do quiet. Or so she thought. The moment Trevor bent his head to take a nipple in his mouth and suckle on it, she gasped so loudly it seemed to echo around them. She grasped his shoulders, biting her lip to stifle a moan. Oh yeah, keeping the noise down was definitely going to be a problem.

Trevor grabbed her gown and pushed it up until he found the tiny scrap of panties underneath. He slipped his hand between her legs to rub her pussy through the thin material.

"Mmm," he breathed. "You're already wet."

Addison could only whimper as he slid a finger in her panties and dipped it into her pussy.

"I need to be inside you," he rasped. "Now."

Addison never made love in the backseat of a car before, and her pulse quickened at the idea. While Trevor unzipped his pants, she wiggled out of her panties and tossed them aside. When his erection sprang free, she stopped to gaze in appreciation for a moment before lifting her gown and straddling his lap.

Placing her hands on his broad shoulders, she slowly lowered herself onto his shaft.

He was hot and hard, and she moaned as he filled her. He felt so good she almost didn't want to move, but Travis cupped her ass, urging her up and down.

"Ride me, baby."

She obediently undulated her hips. He felt so impossibly good inside her, so absolutely perfect. Reaching up, she buried her hands in his hair and tilted his head back so she could kiss him. She plunged her tongue into his mouth, taking possession of it as she rode him a little faster.

"Oh yeah," he murmured against her mouth. "That's it. Ride me."

Although she did as he commanded, Trevor must have thought she needed some encouragement because he gave her ass a hard smack.

She dragged her mouth away from his to look at him, her eyes wide. "I thought we were supposed to be quiet."

He grinned. "Quiet's no fun."

150

He lifted his hand again to smack her on the other cheek. It echoed around them. "Ride me."

She obeyed, moving up and down on his cock in time with his spanks. Heat spread over her ass cheeks, making them tingle. She cooed.

"Harder," she begged.

He complied, delivering a stinging slap to her derriere. "Like that?"

"Yes," she breathed, not caring how loud it was.

And the spanks were loud.

Addison clutched his shoulders, gyrating up and down on him wildly. Each time she came down on his cock, he seemed to go deeper, which only made her move faster. And push her closer and closer to the edge.

With a growl, Trevor grabbed her stinging ass in both hands and thrust up into her. Pleasure surged through Addison, and she buried her face in his neck to stifle her cries of ecstasy. Trevor surged into her and held himself there, his body tightening as he found his own release.

Afterward, Addison collapsed against him, her hand curled around the lapel of his tuxedo. She knew she should climb off his lap and fix her dress, but Trevor's arms felt so good around her that she didn't want to move, not even to cover her nakedness.

She didn't even realize her eyes had drifted closed until Trevor gently shook her shoulder.

"We're home, sweetheart."

Addison smiled. Home. She liked the sound of that.

Reluctantly climbing off his lap, she pulled the gown's straps up over her shoulders just as Bob opened the door for them. That was when she remembered her panties. Just because Leo knew what she and Trevor had been doing back here didn't mean she wanted him finding her underwear when he cleaned the car. She looked around frantically for the garment, finally spotting it wedged in the seat. She reached for them, but Trevor got there first.

Giving her a wink, he picked them up and shoved them in his jacket pocket.

Taking her hand, he helped her out of the limo and swung her up in his arms, told Bob and Leo to have a good night, then carried her into the mansion and up to his bedroom.

It wasn't until they got into bed that Addison realized she still hasn't told Trevor the truth about who she was. Tomorrow, she promised herself. She would definitely tell him tomorrow.

* * *

Something loud and obnoxious sounding woke Addison from a deep, dream-filled sleep the next morning. She lie there for a moment, trying to figure out what it was, but didn't hear it again. Deciding she must have imagined it, she rolled over to snuggle closer to Trevor, but he wasn't in bed.

Still half asleep, she pushed herself up on her elbows, her gaze going to the door to the bathroom. The door was open, but the light was off. He must have gotten up early and decided to let her sleep.

She flopped back on the pillow, thinking about how sweet and considerate he was when the sound of raised voices coming from downstairs made her bolt upright. That must have been the loud, obnoxious sound that had woken her up. Someone was shouting. A woman. Maribel? No, the housekeeper would never yell like that. Who then?

The woman shrieked again, and this time Addison froze.

Oh God. It was Madison.

Oh no! No, no, no, no no!

Addison was out of the bed in a flash. She stopped only long enough to throw a robe on over her naked body before she ran along the hall and hurried down the steps. At

152

the bottom, she skidded to a stop. Her twin sister Madison stood in the middle of the living room, her blonde hair perfectly styled, her designer suit hugging her curves, and her chin lifted indignantly as she faced off against Trevor. Addison had to fight hard not to cringe as Madison turned accusing eyes on her.

"There's my lying, little sister now," Madison sneered.

Addison felt her face color. "Wh-what are you doing here?"

Her twin's blue eyes flashed. "I could ask you the same question. But then I already know the answer." Madison folded her arms. "You're here pretending to be me."

"That isn't true." Addison turned to Trevor. The hurt and betrayal in his eyes brought tears to her own. "This isn't what it looks like, Trevor. I can explain—"

"Oh, come on! It's exactly what it looks like," Madison snarled. "When I changed my mind about being his personal assistant, you decided to take the job instead. I mean, he already had your resume - whoops, my resume - so you figured why the hell not, right?"

"That's enough," Trevor ordered.

"Enough?" Madison let out a harsh laugh. "I'm just getting started." She advanced on Addison. "I couldn't believe it when I got on the internet last night to find you hanging on Trevor Braden's arm, going to movie premieres and getting your photo taken by every paparazzi on the planet. And what am I doing? Picking up some two-hundred-year-old wall street banker's laundry from the dry cleaner in between looking for his damn dentures!"

A tear trickled down Addison's cheek and she angrily wiped it away. "I never told you to take that stupid job in Manhattan. You could have been Trevor's assistant, but you didn't want to babysit some spoiled actor." She saw Trevor lift a brow and gave him an apologetic look. "Those were her words, not mine."

To Addison's surprise, her sister had the decency to look embarrassed. For half a second, at least. "That doesn't give you the right to steal my identity."

"I never stole your identity," Addison insisted. "Not exactly, anyway. I just let Trevor think I was you."

Madison's lip curled. "Semantics, sis. Oh, wait. They probably didn't teach you that word where you went to college, did they?"

Addison ground her jaw. Same old Madison. Still flaunting her Ivy League education in everyone's face. "I don't know why you're so mad. You didn't want the job, so what's the problem? Or are you angry because I finally found something I'm better at than you are?"

"Ha! That'll be the day," Madison scoffed. "You're nothing but a liar and a fraud, and if Trevor Braden won't turn you in to the cops, I will."

Addison's heart lurched. Cops? She'd never considered Trevor might press charges. What she did wasn't really a crime. Was it?

"No one's going to the cops," Trevor said. "Bob, would you mind taking Madison to the gatehouse so I can talk to Addison in private?"

Addison gave herself a mental shake at Bob's name. She hadn't realized the bodyguard was there.

"My pleasure," he said.

Madison took a frantic step back as Bob took a step toward her. "Don't you even think of touching me you big, overgrown pile of muscles. I know Tae-kwon-do."

Bob chuckled. "Me, too. And I'm a lot bigger than you are. Feel free to give it your best shot, though."

Madison held out her hand as if that was supposed to scare Bob off, but he simply picked her up and tossed her over his shoulder. The move not only knocked the breath from her, but loosened her perfect updo, too.

Something Addison would have found amusing if she wasn't so numb. Everything else she'd done since getting here — particularly all the stuff that should have gotten her fired — paled in comparison to this latest transgression.

Giving Addison a wink, Bob turned and headed for the door, Madison beating on his broad back and kicking her legs.

"If you don't put me down right now, I'll have you arrested for assault," she shouted. "I mean it! I'll..."

The rest of her words were lost as Bob disappeared down the hall and into the kitchen. Leaving Addison alone with Trevor. She stared down at the floor, wishing it would open up and swallow her.

"So, this is the big secret Bob said you were keeping from me, isn't it?"

She jerked her head up. "Bob told you?"

"No. He was adamant about it being your secret to tell. He just said whatever it was, it didn't change the fact that you have feelings for me."

"It doesn't." She took a step toward him, then stopped herself. "But it doesn't make what I did okay. My sister might be a stuck-up snob, but she was right about what she said. I used my name, but I still pretended to be her. I didn't go to an Ivy League school like she did. Or work for one of the most prestigious businesses in the country. There was no way I could have gotten this job with my resume. I'm not even remotely as qualified as she is."

Trevor's mouth curved up. "I don't know about that. You seem pretty capable to me. I can't image how Madison would have done better. I know for a fact she wouldn't have figured out Murray was a thief."

"How do you know that?"

"Because she would have been too busy telling me how great she was to notice what anyone else was doing."

He was probably right about that.

She chewed on her lower lip. "Why aren't you mad at me? I lied to you."

"I can't be mad at you. If you hadn't had lied and taken your sister's place, I never would have met you. That would have been the true crime." He reached out to gently brush her hair back. "I need you, Addison. And I'm not just talking about needing you to be my assistant."

She caught her breath at the look in his eyes. "What are you saying, Trevor?"

He cupped her face in his hand. "I'm saying that I love you Addison Mattingly."

She was dreaming, she had to be. But then Trevor bent his head and kissed her, and she knew she wasn't. No kiss in any dream she'd ever had felt this incredible. He honestly, truly loved her.

And while Addison could have stood there in the middle of the living room kissing him for the rest of the day and into the night, she had something important to tell him. So, even though it was hard, she dragged her mouth away from his.

"I love you, too," she said softly. "I have from the moment I first saw you."

She didn't add that she meant the first time she'd seen him on television all those years ago, and thankfully, he didn't ask. Instead, he swung her up in his arms and started up the stairs. She looped her arms around his neck and rested her head on his shoulder, only to jerk upright as a thought occurred to her.

"What about Madison?"

Trevor chuckled. "I'm sure Bob can handle her."

Addison didn't know about that. Her twin was a handful, especially when she was in a mood. But then Addison remembered the way the big bodyguard had tossed her sister over his shoulder. Maybe Madison had finally met her match.

When they got to his bedroom, Trevor set her down and pulled her into his arms for a long, drugging kiss. She clung to him, suddenly unsteady on her feet. He lifted his head with a groan, his hand going to the belt of her robe. She stopped him before he could give it a tug.

"I was wondering..." She hesitated, unable to believe what she'd been about to say.

He slipped his hand beneath her chin, gently lifting her face up when she looked away. "You were wondering what?"

"I was wondering if you could...spank me first?"

There, she'd said it.

Trevor chuckled. "I suppose I could manage it."

He took her hand, probably so he could lead her to the bed, but she hung back.

"I mean a real spanking, like the kind you gave me for messing up when I first started working for you."

He raised a brow.

She blushed. "I know it sounds crazy, but looking back on it I realize that I felt better after you spanked me. Kind of like I was forgiven."

He made small circles on the palm of her hand with his thumb. "I already forgave you for not telling me who you really were, sweetheart."

"I know, but ..." She took a deep breath. "But a spanking would make me feel better. Please."

Trevor regarded her in silence for a long moment. "Okay. If it's what you really want, I'll spank you."

She nodded. "It is."

"Then go into the bathroom and get the hairbrush."

She blinked up at him. "The hairbrush? Why?"

"Because this time, you didn't just spill coffee on a producer or interrupt filming a movie. You lied to me. If I'm going to spank you for it, I want you to remember it so you won't do it again."

Addison's tummy quivered. If she begged him not to use the hairbrush, she was sure he'd relent. But instead of trying to change his mind, she turned and mutely went into the bathroom. Because part of her knew she deserved a harder spanking than he'd ever given her before. And because the other part was a little excited about him using a hairbrush on her poor defenseless bottom.

The brush was on the vanity. It was wood and rectangular in shape, and she couldn't resist smacking it against her palm. She stifled her surprise. Ouch! If it stung that much on her hand, she could only imagine how much more it was going to smart on her ass. Eager to see if she was right, she half turned away from the mirror and was about to give her derriere a smack when Trevor's voice came from the bedroom.

"Are you coming out, or do I need to go in there?"

Addison blushed as much as if he'd walked in and caught her trying to spank herself.

"I'm coming," she called.

Trevor was waiting for her on the couch in the attached sitting room, looking way more relaxed than he had a right to. Her pulse was beating a mile a minute.

Taking a deep breath, Addison walked over to stand in front of him. He didn't say anything, just held out his hand for the brush. She gave it to him, then waited nervously.

"Take off your robe," he commanded softly.

Hands trembling, she slowly untied the belt, then let the robe slip off her shoulders and fall to the floor. Even though she'd been naked in front of him several times already, there was something embarrassing about doing it right before getting spanked, and she flushed.

"Ready?" he asked.

She nodded wordlessly, not trusting herself to speak.

"Climb over my lap."

Addison's color deepened. He was taking this spanking to a whole 'nother level. Well, she'd asked for it.

Avoiding his gaze, she obediently draped herself over Trevor's knee. He placed his hand on her back, holding her in place. She held her breath, tensing as she waited for the hairbrush to connect with her ass. But he surprised her by starting with his hand instead. It wasn't a tender love pat by any means, but it wasn't all that hard, either. She still jumped, though. Which earned her a chuckle and another smack from Trevor.

He spanked one cheek, then the other, going back and forth until her bottom was warm and tingly all over. It felt so good that Addison almost forgot about the hairbrush. Until it smacked against her ass.

"Owwww!" she squealed.

The hairbrush came down on the opposite cheek, this time a little harder. She yelped. It stung way more than his hand.

She lifted her head to look over her shoulder at him. "When I said I wanted you to spank me, I didn't mean this hard."

His mouth quirked. "I'm sure you didn't. But while you were in the bathroom getting the brush I got to thinking about what you did and decided you not only deserve a spanking, but that you need one. So, I'm going to redden your cute, little ass, then I'm going to take you to bed and keep you there until tomorrow."

As delightful as that sounded, she wanted to point out that wasn't very practical. After all, they did have to eat. But Trevor brought the brush down on her ass again. And again. And again.

Addison squirmed and kicked, but Trevor didn't stop. If anything, he spanked her harder. Or maybe it just seemed like that because her ass was on such fire.

Then again, so was her pussy. She was so wet and so hot, she thought she might actually orgasm. But Trevor finished spanking her before she could find out. Giving her two more well-aimed smacks, one to each sit-spot, he pulled her to her feet, swung her up in his arms and carried her over to the bed, where she orgasmed not once, or even twice, but too many times to even count.

* * *

Addison should be as exhausted as Trevor from their lovemaking, but instead she was wide awake. Giddy, even. That wasn't any real surprise. Trevor had just asked him to marry him not five minutes ago.

She glanced over at him as she sat down on the window seat and tucked her legs under her. He was sleeping, a hint of a smile on his handsome face. She smiled, too.

Outside the window, movement caught her attention. She turned to see what it was and was stunned to Madison standing on the front porch of the gatehouse. Her sister was still here? And looking a lot less put together than she had a few hours ago. Her jacket was off, and her hair was hanging loose down her back in a wild tangle.

Even from this distance, Addison could see her twin was angry at whomever she was talking to inside the small cottage. Bob, probably. Poor guy. The things he did for Trevor.

Addison was about to get up and wake Trevor to suggest they go down to the gatehouse and rescue his bodyguard when her sister suddenly reached back with both hands and massaged her bottom. Addison's eyes went wide. If she didn't know better, she'd think Madison had just gotten spanked. Which was ridiculous, of course. If Madison had gotten spanked, she'd run straight to the cops to report whoever had reddened her derriere.

But instead, Madison stood there rubbing what was obviously a very tender backside. Oh yeah, she'd definitely gotten spanked.

Just then, Bob came out onto the porch. He was naked except for a pair of boxer briefs that fit him like a second skin. Addison watched, transfixed as he caught her sister by the hand and pulled her into his arms. She expected Madison to shove him away, maybe even slap his face. But instead, she put her arms around Bob's neck and kissed him back. Seriously.

Addison gasped. Bob and Madison had... Oh God! She couldn't believe it. No way! They couldn't have...

"What are you looking at?" Trevor asked sleepily.

Addison dragged her gaze away from the couple to feast her gaze on her fiancé's bare chest. Whatever was going on between Madison and Bob could wait until later. "Nothing."

"Then come back to bed." He grinned. "We have the whole day to ourselves and I plan on filling every hour of it making love to you."

Laughing, she ran across the room and jumped into bed. "If you insist. I am your personal assistant, after all. If you want spend the day having sex, I'm your girl."

He chuckled and pulled her in for a kiss. "Yes, you are."

The End

Blushing Publications thanks you whole-heartedly for your purchase with us!

There are plenty more stories such as the one you've purchased from Blushing Books! Visit our online store to view our might selection!

http://www.blushingbooks.com

Made in the USA
San Bernardino, CA
04 May 2018